HOLIDAY
HOMICIDE

HOLIDAY HOMICIDE

RUFUS KING

WILDSIDE PRESS

ONE

THE UNKNOWN TROUBADOUR

A nut, if you care to believe it, was the first reason for Cotton Moon getting mixed up on New Year's morning with the homicide in which Myron Jettwick, that prize real-estate operator and heel, starred as the corpse.

The second reason was money; the pay-off being old Miss Emma Jettwick's check for thirty thousand dollars. Moon banked it after her brother's murderer was well on his way toward what an Englishman, who came in on the homestretch of the case down in Tortuagas, called "the heated chair."

Cotton Moon's fees have always come high. They've got to, if he's to stay in that state in which he has decided to keep himself. Also if he wants to go plowing about the seven seas on his boat *Coquilla* in search of rare nuts to add to his collection, and sometimes eat. You cannot push one hundred and fifty feet of expensive steel and a crew of eighteen men about in the water on charity. Moon informed me of that truism when he first employed me six years ago as his assistant. He claims that he hired me because he had never before found a bartender who could take dictation and type, as well as swing the more permanent of the stiffs out of a waterfront bar at closing time. He said that by doing so he was also removing a faint blemish from the bartender union's escutcheon.

Whether that was an insult or not I've still got to find out.

The nut which started off the business on New Year's morning was not a peanut or a chestnut which, according to Moon, are like having grits for breakfast instead of one of Walter's omelets. Walter is *Coquilla*'s cook and was absorbed by Moon, among other things, in Madagascar. The nut was a sapucaia nut, and it hit Moon on the forehead as we were standing on *Coquilla*'s aft-deck and greeting the first morning of the year through a seven-o'clock murk and snow which were tenting New York City's East River.

It looked to me like any plain Brazil nut when I picked it up, but Moon said no. It was a sapucaia, and was rare enough in the fruit shops of New York to be practically extinct. The same held true in its native Brazil where it was produced by a big tree called *Lecthis ollaria* or, if you had to, plain cannon-ball tree.

Its name came from the large urn-shaped capsules which the Brazilians called monkey-pots and which held the nuts. Its scarcity on the home lot was caused by the continual race between the monkeys and the Brazilians to get the nuts, with the monkeys winning hands down as they had the added advantage of tails.

It was a smooth-shelled nut, except for a few deep longitudinal wrinkles, and its color was a heavy amber brown. Moon told me to eat it, which I did, and found the flavor something like that of an almond, only sweeter.

Just about then a voice from the landing stage called up:

"I'm sorry, but I'm nervous and you were nothing but a blur. I didn't mean to hit you. I was standing in the bows of the *Trade Wind* and letting of steam."

Trade Wind was moored to the landing stage of Wharf House, just aft of *Coquilla*. She was a smart-looking tub, a two-hundred-footer, and we knew she belonged to Myron Jettwick, although we didn't know right then that Myron Jettwick was dead. Wharf House itself was Jettwick's last building development. It covered three city blocks of the East River waterfront, and Moon kept an apartment in it because it had a place to hitch up boats to.

We went to the starboard railing and looked down on the voice. It belonged to a decently built young fellow wrapped in a quilted wool dressing gown that reminded me of one I'd seen recently in a mid-town store tagged at one hundred and twenty-five dollars. This was on over heavy silk pajamas of a real violent yellow color, and there was nothing on his feet but those thin leather slippers which come in a case and are given to you by aunts at Christmas to be used in Pullmans.

The fact that several inches of wet snow covered the landing stage and that the temperature was below freezing didn't seem to have occurred to him at all.

"Have you ever," Moon asked him, "considered pneumonia?"

"Why not? Or is river water better?"

"Entirely a point of view. But it happens to be the year's happiest morning. Why die?"

I suggested having Walter mix one of his pick-me-ups which are based on raw eggs stifled in Tabasco and brandy, but Moon signaled me to keep quiet and I knew, then, that the problem was more desperate than a plain hangover, if anything can be.

"I don't want to die unless I have to," young Desperate said, "but there's a very good chance of the warden at Sing Sing issuing invitations for my going-out party, and it's a method of departure that doesn't appeal. Where are all the cops in this town anyhow?"

"They are attempting to survive the wake held last night on the old year. Why?"

"Because McRoss called the police about fifteen minutes ago, and nothing's happened. McRoss is Jettwick's secretary, or was. Jettwick's dead. Somebody shot him last night and killed him. I'm his stepson and also his nephew, whichever you like. Me, I don't like either."

"Come aboard, Mr. Jettwick. This flirting with pulmonary pneumonia is absurd."

Moon turned to me and said, "Spiced toddies if you please, Bert, in the main saloon. Ask Walter to make them with the Demerara rum."

I rooted out Walter, who was in the galley drinking coffee, and gave him the order. It called for one half lump of sugar, one jigger of Demerara rum, a half bar-spoonful of allspice and the balance boiling water, to each. That was the way Moon liked them.

Then I went into the main saloon.

Jettwick was shivering the way you do after staying in cold ocean water too long, and anyone could see that it wasn't a physical chill, but that his nerves were all shot.

"This is my secretary, Bert Stanley," Moon said, "Mr. Bruce Jettwick."

We shook hands, and young Jettwick's grip was good, even though the effect was something like squeezing a fillet of tough mullet fresh off the ice.

"Bert, you have heard Mr. Jettwick sing. He is professionally billed on the radio as the Unknown Troubadour, and has been featured during the past year on he Violet Vane Cosmetic Hour."

"'Has been' is good."

"Mr. Jettwick is afraid that being involved in a murder investigation will not help to advance his career. Obviously, he is right."

"Can you catch the announcer?" Jettwick's voice was good and bitter. "'I give you now the Unknown Troubadour, whose identity has been exposed over a nationwide publicity hookup during his recent sojourn at the Tombs, while on trial for the murder of his uncle. He will sing as his first number *The Prisoner's Song*, to remind you that when it comes to removing your prison pallor, Violet Vane face lotions will do the trick.' Well, nuts."

"Just so, Mr. Jettwick. Where did you get them? I refer to the sapucaias, with one of which you hit me on the head."

"Oh, those. A friend sends them up to me from Rio de Janeiro."

"They should not be thrown carelessly about."

"I said that I was sorry, Mr. Moon."

"Not that: I mean because of their rarity."

"In the spot that I'm in, I've no time to worry about the rarity of any nuts."

Moon let some of his native Virginia gentleness get into his voice.

"It wasn't you who, by any chance or accident, shot your uncle, was it, Mr. Jettwick?"

"No, unfortunately; but I'd have liked to. My trouble is that I only remembered half an hour ago about that damned silver mirror."

Walter brought in the hot spiced rums, and Moon told young Jettwick to drink one of them and calm down, and under no circumstances ever to admit to a willingness to have committed a murder which has just been done. Jettwick had no idea, Moon said, how refreshing any district attorney found statements like that. They grabbed them up with the avidity of a woman at a sale of imported bags.

Moon was still in the process of handing out good, and so far free, advice when a deck steward brought in a nice-faced old lady all bundled up in sables.

She went right over to young Jettwick and sat down beside him on the settee. Her voice had a clear Western tone to it as she said:

"Bruce dear, the police are on board. You must come back."

He introduced us.

"My aunt, Miss Jettwick, Mr. Stanley, and Mr. Cotton Moon."

You could see Miss Jettwick's bright nice eyes grow sharply interested.

"Mr. Moon? Didn't you handle that mess for Amy Bettling down at Santa Monica last year?"

Moon said that he had. It had netted him twenty-one thousand dollars, and had kept Mrs. Roger Bettling's redheaded daughter Eunice from a neat extortion. She had had a yen for trombone players, and probably still has. It had also helped to buy fuel oil for hustling *Coquilla* after some *Aleurites triloba* down in the South Seas. You called them candle nuts after you got to know them better, and Moon liked to make night lights out of their oil.

"I suppose my nephew has told you that my brother has been shot?"

"Yes. My sympathies, Miss Jettwick."

"Thank you. What I would really like, Mr. Moon, would be your help."

Moon never beats about the bush. He said:

"My minimum price for a murder investigation is thirty thousand dollars, above any expenses involved." It was a sale.

TWO

THE SILVER MIRROR

Moon wanted some plain facts, while a steward was going for our coats and a pair of galoshes for Bruce Jettwick.

I got my book and took notes, being conscious, as always, of the faintly surprised expression in Moon's eyes. He says that I still put down pothooks with the rhythm of a shakerful of cocktails being iced.

"Miss Jettwick, we will start with the crime. I know that your brother has been shot; that is all."

There was an absence of any grief about her brother's violent death in that steady Western voice of hers; not markedly so, as it had been with Bruce, but the absence was there just the same.

"A sailor was clearing the snow from a small aft-deck that goes around my brother's quarters on the *Trade Wind*. He noticed that the lights were on, and looked in through a porthole. He saw Myron, and saw that Myron had been killed, and shouted out."

"What time was this?"

"I think about six-thirty."

"Where was your brother's body?"

"Myron was sitting up on the bed. I've seen—I mean, I went inside the bedroom after Mr. Talbot told me, and it was pretty ghastly."

"Mr. Talbot?"

"He is one of the officers. I think the sailor started for the bridge and met Mr. Talbot running down because of the shout. They both went back to Myron's quarters, and by that time most of us were out in the passageway of the cabin deck, and Mr. Talbot came and told us what had happened."

"Did Mr. Talbot use a passkey, or was the door to your brother's quarters unlocked?"

"It was unlocked. Captain Plummet had joined us by then, and he got in touch with the police. I dressed."

She turned her nice bachelor-button eyes on Bruce. "I missed you. A sailor said he had seen you come aboard here, so I came over too."

"Anything else, Miss Jettwick?"

"No, not that I can think of right now."

"And you, Mr. Jettwick? You spoke of a silver mirror bothering you. How?"

"Because I held it close to Myron's nose to see if he were alive."

"When? After the sailor had discovered the crime?"

"No, after I had discovered it myself, at three o'clock this morning."

You had to like the way Miss Jettwick took this in her stride. It was a shock to her, but she didn't go to pieces.

You could almost see her hack stiffening beneath the sable coat, and her voice didn't miss a beat as she said: "Don't worry, Bruce."

"I didn't think of the mirror until half an hour ago. Naturally my fingerprints must be all over it. Next time I'll wear gloves."

"Mr. Jettwick," Moon said sharply, "I repeat that that sort of an attitude has its danger. I advise strongly that you stop it. Tell me exactly what happened."

"The boat phone in my cabin rang a few minutes before three. A voice said. 'This is Myron.' He wanted me to come right back to his quarters. I finished a cigarette, which took a few minutes, and then went back. My uncle was sitting up in the bed, shot in the head."

"Was the wound still bleeding?"

"No, but the blood hadn't coagulated, if that's what you mean."

"I do. Be more exact, if you can, as to the time that elapsed between the phone call and your arrival in your uncle's quarters."

"Well, the cigarette was almost finished when the phone rang. I'd say maybe three minutes, or five at the most."

"Now that you can look back on it, was the imitation of your uncle's voice over the boat telephone convincing? Since the blood had stopped flowing, the voice was obviously an impersonation."

"I don't know. I wasn't familiar with his voice. I'd never heard it over a telephone, and we'd only spoken a few words together last night. I hadn't seen him until then since I was ten years old."

"We will consider that later, Mr. Jettwick. Your movements of the moment, if you please. Open your uncle's door and go on from there."

"The door is at the end of the passageway, and opens into the living room."

"Did you knock?"

"Yes, but there wasn't any answer so I went right in."

"Lights?"

"They were all on."

"Was the furniture in order?"

"Yes, there weren't any signs of a disturbance. I saw an open door and went over to it. It was the bedroom door, and he was on the bed."

"Were the lights on in there too?"

"Yes, all of them."

"Was he lying on top of the covers or beneath them?"

"He was under the covers, sort of sitting up and propped against the pillows. It knocked me out for a minute; I mean, just having heard his voice and then finding him dead like that."

"Try and remember clearly every move you made."

"I went over to him and tried to feel his pulse."

"Was the wrist warm? Flexible?"

"Yes, it was warm, and very loose. Then I saw a mirror on the bureau and tried to see if his breath would cloud it. It didn't."

"Have you had much experience with the determination of death?"

"None. But you read about mirrors and such simple tests. My father, Myron's brother, was run over and killed by a taxicab in Vienna when I was nine. That's the only other time I've ever seen anyone dead."

"What did you do with the silver mirror?"

"I put it back on the bureau. I felt sick."

"Did you search your uncle's quarters for his attacker?"

"No, I just felt sick, so I went back to my cabin and was."

"Did you meet any one of the crew or of your party in the passageway?"

"No, no one."

"We can presume that the murderer used a silencer, or else that the general racket of the New Year's Eve celebration baffled the sound of the shot. Why didn't you give the alarm at once?"

"I don't know. I was just too sick, I guess."

Moon's voice lost its touch of Virginia softness and moved several states north.

"Mr. Jettwick, if I am to help you I cannot countenance evasions. You are not speaking to the police when you speak to me. I am being paid to help you, not to convict you, although I shall cheerfully do so should my investigation point to your guilt. You arc not a weakling, either physically or morally. That is apparent. I believe that you did not search for the murderer and you did not give the alarm because you thought you knew who had shot your uncle. Am I right?"

"No."

Moon shrugged.

"I am sorry, Miss Jettwick, but I must withdraw from the case."

"Bruce dear." Emma Jettwick's small hand looked like a white leaf on Bruce's big one. "It's Helen, isn't it? You were thinking of Helen?"

Bruce kept on looking sullen and desperate, which is easy when you've got a brush of dark hair and strong, homely features. It's only the blonds who get no place when they try it. But he didn't take his hand away from under hers.

Finally he said:

"Yes, and I wouldn't have blamed her. I had my gun along to do it myself. After I got sensible again I knew she never could have done it, because she never would have telephoned me to come back there and get involved. She'd have killed herself first."

"Helen," Miss Jettwick said, "is Bruce's mother. Surely, Mr. Moon, you will reconsider?"

Moon jumped back across the Mason and Dixon line. "I will do so only, as I have stated before, if there are no further evasions."

"I've got no more evasions," Bruce said.

"Very well, go back to the point from where you left your uncle's quarters."

"I went to Mother's cabin and we talked the thing over. She was as upset as I was, and I guess we talked for an hour or so but there didn't seem to be any answer, except to keep still and see what happened. Mother told me to go back to my cabin and get undressed. That was around five o'clock. We planned to wait until the body was found, and then act surprised like the rest. Well, all that was all right until I remembered the mirror."

"You say undress. You had not gone to bed?"

"No."

"This gun that you took with you, have you a police permit for it?"

"Yes."

You could tell from Moon's expression that he thanked God for that small mercy.

"On what grounds was the permit issued you?"

"My agent arranged it. He's Ben Wolf."

"When did you get the permit?"

"Two weeks ago."

"I repeat, on what grounds?"

"Pull. Ben Wolf can get anything."

"Why did you want this gun?"

Young Jettwick found the old favorite groove again.

"To shoot my uncle with, if I had to. If I had to stop him from ruining Mother's life once more, and mine."

"Splendid."

"I'm only saying this to you, Mr. Moon. You wanted no evasions."

Moon let that limp look cover his eyes while he stared through a porthole at slow-falling flakes of snow, and the room was quiet except for small noises which the tide made as the river pressed past *Coquilla*'s port side.

I knew he was trying to make up his mind whether to take a chance on a client talking himself into an electrical exit, or to give up the case plus its thirty thousand dollars. The dollars would have made a contemplated run down to Guiana after some Pekea nuts so much velvet. Moon wanted the Pekea nuts very badly, to use in a recipe for a new soup, and the nuts won. He stayed on the case.

"Who is on board the *Trade Wind*, Miss Jettwick?' he asked.

"We've two guests, Harriet Schuyler and her daughter Elizabeth. They were to be with us for several weeks at Myron's place on Tortuagas, in the Caribbean. Then there are Bruce and his mother, of course, and Myron's secretary, Jepson McRoss."

I remembered a picture of Elizabeth Schuyler in the *Tribune* a few weeks ago. I remembered it because you could see a slight difference between it and the pictures of four other debutantes on the same page. There was less expensive fog about it, and the re-toucher had actually left a suggestion of a chin.

She had come out the night before the picture was printed, in a brawl thrown by her mother at the Waldorf, and it struck me as funny that she'd leave town during the height of her first season for a cruise to the Caribbean with a radio singer and his mother and a real-estate operator who was now a corpse.

Moon found it funny, too, although he seemed more interested in Mrs. Schuyler's reason than in the girl's.

"I believe that Mrs. Schuyler is interested in real estate," he said. "Would you have called her a rival of your brother's, Miss Jettwick?"

"A friendly one, yes. Their tactics were quite different. Myron would consider a possible project down to its least detail, whereas Mrs. Schuyler has been known to plunge her whole fortune blindly on some development that struck her fancy."

"Were you all on board last night?"

"Yes. We had planned to sail around nine o'clock this morning."

The steward came back with our coats and the galoshes for Bruce. Moon said to Bruce while he was putting them on:

"Mr. Jettwick, when we board the *Trade Wind* I think you will find yourself faced by District Attorney John Seward. The people involved are important enough to have him handle the case himself. I am glad of it, because he is a just man and a sensible one. In view of your fingerprints on the silver mirror you have no alternative other than to tell him the exact truth. Be good enough to make just one reservation: ignore your real reason for having taken out a license for carrying a gun. I imagine that your salary as a featured star in radio was a large one?"

"I got two thousand a week."

"In that case we will presume that you are in the habit of carrying large sums in cash, a fact possibly known to the more predatory habitués of the town's night clubs. You felt the need of protection, hence the gun. It smacks of evasion, but not provably so. Your safety lies on one thing: the fact that your uncle was dead when you reached his quarters in answer to that deceptive telephone call. I refer to your safety from immediate arrest. Ultimately, of course, it lies in my unmasking the person who committed the crime. Let us go."

THREE

LAMB OR WOLF

Something should have warned me the minute we hit the deck of *Trade Wind* that there was going to be more trouble.

Just as Mrs. Roger Bettling's daughter, Eunice, out in Santa Monica had had red hair, so did Elizabeth, this young prize of Harriet Schuyler's, have red hair—only redder, and with some yellow gold in it. She was wearing it the way it had been in the *Tribune* picture, off the ears, and with that crown-roast effect which passed at the time for sophistication and was death on hats.

Her face had the regulation number of features, and would have been a distinct pleasure to look at if she had wiped off the careworn, haggard look of seventeen which, she later told me, was imperative for a girl's first season.

She had picked out a woolen dress of arsenical Paris green, and a short mink jacket, with muff, as the suitable sort of a costume to start a murder investigation off with a bang. We found her standing by the gangplank when we came aboard, exchanging reminiscences with a hard-faced cop in uniform who was trying to make up his mind whether or not he should look shocked.

It needed no chart to discover that she and Bruce had passed the stage of checking up on mutual acquaintances, common likes and dislikes, and were well on their way toward calling each other by their middle names. This astonished me when I found out that they'd only met each other the night before, but my brief years as a bartender had given me small opportunity for examining the antics of young love.

The examples I'd been used to were mostly exploited by disappointed male turkeys, on the other side of the bar in Harrigan's waterfront tavern. They had systematically tried to drown their sorrows in drink and a fine flow of four-letter words arranged in epitaph formation for the current tramp who was double-timing them with some wiper off a sister ship.

In spite of the color of Elizabeth Schuyler's hair I felt that this was going to be different and even looked forward, like a fool, to seeing romance unfold.

Miss Jettwick introduced us.

Coming through the river smells you could catch an impressive short-jab from the perfume that operated from the arsenical green wool and mink. It was called Flaming Sin, and rated eighteen dollars an ounce in an enameled flacon shaped like an apple.

Moon, who can take young love or leave it, was more interested in finding out the official setup. The hard-faced cop told him that District Attorney Seward was on board, Chief Medical Examiner Dutton, Assistant Police Commissioner McGilvray and the usual cast of bright young things from the homicide squad.

We followed Miss Jettwick into *Trade Wind*'s main saloon.

A man was sitting there alone. Miss Jettwick went over to him and said:

"Wallace, so good of you to come, so thoughtful. Do you know Mr. Cotton Moon, Mr. Wallace Emberry?" I got the name at once. Emberry held a high position in the Bar Association of the state and I judged, which was right, that he had been Myron Jettwick's lawyer. Anybody would have mistaken him, on first sight, for an Englishman. His whole appearance suggested county, moors, heather, and the better hunts, and you could make a safe bet that the slight bulge around his middle was the result of a daily diet of steak-and-kidney pies. However, his record at the bar was smart enough so that he could get away with it, even to the accent which out-Harrowed Harrow.

Emberry found one of Miss Jettwick's hands, pressed it between both of his and said:

"McRoss telephoned me. Naturally I came at once. What a brutal shock this has been."

"Very, Wallace."

His focus widened and took in Moon.

"We've never met, Mr. Moon, but I have followed your career with the greatest interest and admiration. Your handling of that Harkness Stone business here two years ago was masterly. I wonder whether Miss Jettwick has been wise, and has persuaded you to interest yourself in this regrettable business?"

"Miss Jettwick has, although the wisdom remains to be seen."

"Nonsense, it was the greatest stroke of luck to have found you within reach."

This social chitchat was quickly interred, and Moon sent a steward with his compliments to District Attorney Seward, and a request that we be permitted to take a look at the scene of the crime.

Moon didn't waste the interval while the steward was gone. He said:

"Mr. Emberry, were you familiar with Myron Jettwick's financial condition as of, to put it bluntly, yesterday?"

Emberry showed a lot of strong white teeth and thickened his English accent a little to catch Moon, who was back again in Virginia.

"Naturally, Mr. Jettwick had his reserves, even from me. Offhand I should say that his finances were excellent. He had the Midas touch, if you don't mind the cliché. Personally, I like clichés and find them most soothing. They have the warm effect of dust on a fine painting. Wasn't it Whistler who said it should never be removed?"

Moon didn't know, and said so, and then asked Emberry if he knew who would benefit, financially, by Myron Jettwick's death. Emberry again found Miss Jettwick's hand and pressed it.

"You," he said. "Myron left everything to you, Emma. He has even named you his sole executor, to serve without bond."

Miss Jettwick's nice Western voice was anything but overwhelmed by gratitude or surprise.

"I'm sorry," she said. "I wish that he had felt and done differently."

This made no sense at the time, and Moon didn't check up on it until later because the steward came back right then and said that the district attorney would be glad to have us join him. We would find him in Myron Jettwick's quarters on the cabin deck.

Moon followed the steward, and I followed Moon.

We left Miss Jettwick and Wallace Emberry going into a huddle in one corner of the main saloon, and Bruce and Elizabeth Schuyler in a denser huddle in another. I heard Elizabeth saying as I passed her:

"Certainly I believe that people have the right to kill for cause. But why be stupid about it? Why a gun?"

It sounded fearfully modern and all that, but her seventeen years stuck out all over her, and you knew at heart that she was nothing but a scared kid, and that Bruce was one, too, in spite of his practically senile outlook of twenty-four.

Say what you will, it is next to impossible to get used to the sight of a death by violence. The impersonal and businesslike front put on by the boys from Center Street doesn't mean a thing. It is constantly messy, unpleasant, and a shock.

Myron Jettwick's body was no exception. The bullet had smacked in just above the right temple and a liver-blue streak ran down over paste-colored skin, while there was something surprised and childish about the expression on that absolutely still, old face.

Moon greeted everybody, and was greeted back.

Then he and the district attorney and I left the bedroom to its crush of officially busy bees, and moved into the living room of the suite. It was empty, except for a plain-clothes man in an ash-gray fedora who had deduced the location of a bottle of Courvoisier, a humidor filled with Corona Coronas, and nothing else.

Seward chased him out.

Seward had just got back with his wife and two kids from a short vacation in Bermuda, and Moon asked him the usual questions about how he'd liked it, and whether he'd frozen to death, and how were the planters' punches holding up, and whether the turtle was still eating flaming hibiscus petals in the patio halfway up the hill in Hamilton, and it was all most social except that Moon's eyes never left the few exhibits that had already been collected, and which were spread out on a table near which we were sitting.

The silver hand mirror was there, all right, carefully protected for transportation down to the identification bureau in makeshift crating made from strips of wood from a cigar box. The fingerprints hadn't been developed as yet, but they must have been plainly visible in an indirect light because of the smooth hardness of the mirror's surface.

There were six water glasses, similarly protected and tagged, and obviously from the bathrooms of the five guests and the secretary, McRoss.

There was a dress shirt with a small brown stain on its starched white cuff, waiting to turn out as human blood after a chemical test. Embroidered on one sleeve were the initials: B. J.

The last exhibit, also tagged, was an opened box of revolver cartridges. Even with the reports in from just these few districts it began to look like a landslide for young Jettwick.

Moon believes in attack.

"I can save you a little bother, Mr. Seward," he said. "The prints on that silver hand mirror were left there by my client, Bruce Jettwick, at three o'clock this morning. He was trying to determine whether or not his uncle was dead."

Moon leaned over and fingered labels.

"The prints will check with the ones on this glass."

Seward took this very nicely. He has a pleasant face, very gentlemanly, and strictly on the poker order except for his smile, which is agreeable to look at but doesn't mean anything at all.

"I suppose," he said, flashing the smile, "your client wanted to make certain that he had done a good job?"

"Naturally. He will give you a statement to that effect himself."

"Just a nice Greek bearing a gift?"

"Not only a gift, but a gun. I presume those cartridges were taken from his stateroom? I am delighted to say that he has a police permit for it, and can prophesy with the utmost conviction that when the murder bullet is removed at the post mortem the ballistic expert will announce that it does not correspond with a test bullet fired from my client's gun."

"He is beginning to sound like a lamb fitted out with the accessories of a wolf."

"He is a lamb, Mr. Seward. I refer to him in his complete innocence, not pictorially. It is my intention to see that he is not shorn."

The bell rang on round one.

FOUR

THE BUSINESS OF THE HAT

The arena moved to the dining saloon on the deck above.

Nobody had had any breakfast, and Miss Jettwick, being a wise woman as well as an exceedingly nice one, knew very well the physiological link between the temper centers of the human body and its stomach. She sent a steward to request that the district attorney and Moon and I join her.

Assistant Police Commissioner McGilvray and Chief Medical Examiner Dutton were also included in the invitation, but refused on the grounds of a more pressing engagement. Miss Jettwick, very shortly, had a buffet breakfast set up in a cabin adjacent to the scene of the crime for them and the boys to snack at while they worked. It stopped the investigation for a solid half-hour.

The three other principals in the cast were in the dining saloon when we got there. It was a pleasant room, paneled in Circassian walnut, and warm with a blending of expensive perfumes and the smell of good hot coffee.

Elizabeth's mother was easy to spot. She had that set, enameled glint of any mother of any New York debutante who has either just paid the coming-out bills, or else is wondering how she is going to do it. Mrs. Schuyler's glint must have cost around twenty thousand dollars, judging from the account in Nicky Manhattan's column of the champagne tidal wave that had broken the dam at the Waldorf. Otherwise Mrs. Schuyler was as easy to look at as her daughter, and seemed far, far better preserved.

Bruce's mother was a different matter. If you were to put a woman through a wringer, and then starch her to stiffen her up, you might get some idea of what I mean. There was no dying swan about her, or Camille, or Mimi, or anything like that; it was simply that she looked like a sleek motor job that's been in a bad traffic accident and has been put together again too quick.

As for Jepson McRoss, he was harder to figure out, and a single look at him gave him my vote for Suspect Number One. All he needed was a good dark night and an opera cloak, and watch him go to town. Which shows how wrong you can be sometimes, and sometimes how right. His face lacked a waxed black mustache and nothing else, but his wavy dark hair made up for it, and it was a cinch that anybody who cared to sink a well in its locks would strike oil.

Miss Jettwick dealt out the introductions, and I found myself seated between Spider McRoss and Mrs. Schuyler, and in front of a handsome plate of baked kidneys, Canadian bacon and potatoes hashed to a brown that would have turned Walter's face white with envy.

For the sake of everybody's digestion, Seward started a general conversation based on his stay in Bermuda. This lasted brightly through the first cup of coffee, and then expired.

Mrs. Schuyler nailed the lid shut by saying:

"I dined with Sir Alfred at Government House when Elizabeth and I were there last April. Such pleasant marines, or were they orderlies, Elizabeth? So difficult to translate them into footmen. Subconsciously, I was waiting for them to present arms with the soup. The point is, Mr. Seward, that it must have been a perfect vacation for a man in your profession. Sir Alfred told me that the island was perennially bothered by rain, drunken tourists, and flies, yes, but *never* by murder."

Seward's smile brightened the sudden fog.

"Oh, I believe there have been a few exceptions," he said.

"Well, of course, if you care to include that colored man who pushed his children down a well. But that's different, wouldn't you say? I mean, it's so racial."

Spider McRoss didn't help out any, either. His voice, if you could have touched it, would have felt like a better quality silk.

"In any community, no matter how confined by natural barriers, or how small, there is always murder. I'm unfamiliar with the census number of the population that surrounded Cain and Abel but I imagine it must have been quite negligible, or does anybody know?"

Wallace Emberry was sitting across the table from me. He looked at McRoss coldly, and said in his best courtroom voice:

"Shall we settle on twelve? Say seven adults, of assorted sex, and five children?"

The fog thickened.

"I do think it's stupid to temporize." This was Miss Jettwick speaking. "There's only one thing on our minds, and that's Myron's murder. And, apart from the tragedy of his passing, we're naturally wondering how it's going to affect all of us here. Let's talk about it frankly. Shall we, Mr. Seward, or would you prefer to wait?"

"I believe later, Miss Jettwick. Less collectively, don't you think? That is, unless one of you has some information that I should know of at once?"

We could have finished our kidneys in peace after this, if Mrs. Schuyler hadn't begun to rattle. She gave us her best madam-president voice and said:

"I know precisely what you mean, Mr. Seward. The odd things, the little things that seem of no importance to a layman's mind, but which a trained detective instantly clarifies into an essential clue. Wasn't it an inappropriate necktie that trapped that horrible optometrist last year? I mean, the murdered man's wife felt that nobody but a blind man would select that color tie to go with the color shirt the optometrist was wearing, and spoke to the police about it?"

Seward, under his polite smile, was plainly interested, and I could see that Moon was, too, from the way his fingers tightened a little on the handle of his cup.

"Yes, Mrs. Schuyler, the man was color-blind and the tie incident did help to solve the case. Naturally, with things like that, the wheat is infrequent and there is a good deal of chaff."

"Naturally. I would consider as chaff, for example, the fact that when we gathered in the passageway after the sailor shouted his alarm, Bruce's hair wasn't tousled from sleep, but carefully brushed. I dismissed the fact at once on the grounds of his being an artist. My deduction being that no artist under any circumstances would ever appear in public with his hair uncombed."

The fog was by now pea soup. We all caught the effect, in that dominant voice, of direct attack. There was no time to pin a reason for it because Helen Jettwick was suddenly stung into dropping a depth bomb of her own. She had been sitting perfectly quietly beside Bruce, just looking starched and wrung out and deadly pale.

"That must have been the second time you looked out into the passageway, Mrs. Schuyler? I believe the hour was about half past six when the sailor's shout brought us from our cabins, that is, all but you?"

Harriet Schuyler's arm jerked sharply against mine, and I had to spear another kidney.

"Really? I rather remember, Mrs. Jettwick, that I joined the rest of you at once."

"No, not at once. I'm certain that I caught a glimpse of you standing in your cabin doorway. Then you closed the door for a moment. When you opened it again, this time to join us, you had removed your hat."

Well, I have always said that nothing can be more lethal in a nice way than a nice woman when she turns tiger in defense of her young. I saw Moon's expression change slightly as he glanced at Mrs. Schuyler and then back again to Helen Jettwick, and knew that he was figuring the same thing, too.

If I, with my slender experience in such matters and having no blood connection whatever, had been able to see that Bruce and Elizabeth were going down for the third time about each other, it was a sure thing that Harriet Schuyler and Helen Jettwick hadn't missed it either.

Still, there they were,, coming right out in meeting, with Mrs. Schuyler hinting at dirty work on the part of Mrs. Jettwick's hopeful because of a hair comb, and with Mrs. Jettwick practically accusing her son's hoped-to-be-mother-in-law of grim intentions by being dressed and having her hat on at six-thirty in the morning. Bruce's hair business didn't matter, as we were willing to admit that he had stayed up all night anyway, but that hat business was fishy enough to smell like Gloucester.

To say that Seward was interested was putting it mildly. Moon, of course, was entranced.

Not so, however, either Bruce or Elizabeth. Bruce just stared at his mother and looked stunned, as if she'd taken off a mask or something. As for Elizabeth, she stopped looking haggard and careworn, and looked a plain seventeen that has just been given a good slap. She looked quickly at Helen Jettwick, then at her mother, and then not so quickly at Bruce. And as glazed writers say, there came into her eyes an expression which boded him ill. Seward said politely:

"I am sure that Mrs. Schuyler will have a perfectly reasonable explanation for the hat."

She had.

"We were to sail at nine this morning," she said. "We had planned to be gone from the city for an absence of several weeks. Are you aware, Mr. Seward, of my operations in real estate?"

"Yes. I think your latest venture was that apartment block near Columbia University?"

"Precisely. For indigent students. Unhappily it became completely tenanted by modest business couples. I can do nothing about it, as the property yields around twenty-two percent. I shall devise another project for the students. It is important that they be taken out of unimaginative rooming houses and sympathetically housed."

Still nothing about hats. Seward brought her graciously back to them by simply saying:

"And the hat?"

"I required some data that I had left at home. I suddenly remembered it this morning on waking. I required it to discuss with Myron Jettwick on this trip. It consists of notes in a small notebook which I had left in my desk. I dressed, and was prepared to take a taxi home to get it, when that seaman screamed."

It was thin. In fact, it stuck out like bare bones in the silence that followed the stopping of Mrs. Schuyler's voice.

Just how thin it was, none of us realized completely until McRoss later told us about the black steel box.

FIVE

THE BLACK STEEL BOX

Moon has a flair for selecting the one person in a group who can give him the quickest digest of all angles on a situation. In picking out McRoss he made no mistake.

Our gay little group had broken up immediately after breakfast. Seward had suggested to Mrs. Schuyler that they go below and keep right on discussing real estate and hats, especially from the angle of her having taken the hat off.

Wallace Emberry and Miss Jettwick wanted to talk about the arrangements for her brother's funeral, and Miss Jettwick asked Helen Jettwick to be with them while they did so.

Bruce and Elizabeth scattered as far away from each other as the boat allowed. Both went out on deck, and he courted another bout with pneumonia in the bows while she went back to the taffrail and consented to pose for a few tragic press photographs for the first arrivals among the reporters, who were kept in herd on the landing stage under the eyes of the hard-faced cop.

Moon and I followed McRoss into a small library on the main deck. I got out my notebook, and Moon got right down to business.

"Mr. McRoss, just how closely were you in Mr. Jettwick's confidence?"

McRoss said he had often wondered. He tried to explain.

"You always felt a sense of complete intimacy when you were with him," he said. "It had a conspiratorial touch, though, rather than one of candor. I mean, he not only told you things, but he seemed to involve you in them just by telling you about them."

"His business record establishes him as having been a remarkably astute man."

"He was."

"Were you with him for long?"

"No, simply during the past three years."

"It's astonishing how unastute such men can frequently be in their private lives. They can face an economic problem with precision, and still bog down helplessly among the human equations. Did you find that true with Mr. Jettwick?"

"True? Oh, but decidedly so. Just take his divorced wife and her son, for an example."

"Let's," said Moon.

"Do you know anything about it? The divorce, I mean?"

"No."

"It wasn't nice. The papers were full of it fifteen years ago. She married Myron's younger brother Alfred first. I'm speaking of Helen Jettwick, of course. Bruce was born, and I think he was about nine years old when Alfred Was killed in Vienna by a taxicab. Then she married Myron. Am I clear?"

"Quite, thank you."

"Well, that only lasted for a year. They honeymooned in Africa, and came back to the States on the *Leviathan*. That's when things started. It's hard to believe it when you look at her, but you never can tell when you go by faces, can you?"

"Tell what, Mr. McRoss?"

"Tell whether or not a person has criminal tendencies. She looks like such a *nice* woman, but there it was. She stole some valuable jewelry from the wife of a Senator Blackman during the crossing. The customs found it stuffed in a toe of a slipper when they went through her things on the dock, and Mrs. Blackman insisted on prosecuting. Wallace Emberry handled the case for Helen Jettwick, incidentally. He was Myron Jettwick's lawyer even back in those days, and he did get her off with a suspended sentence. There was the worst sort of publicity, and then the divorce came along to finish it."

"Because of the theft?"

"Oh, no. It was worse than that. You can imagine how the relationship between Myron and her was, well, strained. It isn't as if he didn't stand by her, because he did. It seems that he almost bent backward being noble about it, and I daresay they'd have just agreed to a quiet separation if it hadn't been for Jeffry Smith."

"Mr. Smith became the third leg of a triangle?"

"Yes, exactly. I understand he was a rotter if there ever was one, and even Mr. Jettwick's nobility snapped under the strain and he divorced her. If you look up the papers you'll find it was one of the messiest divorces on record. Social ostracism puts it mildly. I mean that she and Bruce vanished at once into some sort of a limbo that must have been appalling, especially in those days when sin was sin. You remember the era?"

"Perfectly, Mr. McRoss."

"Then came this business of two weeks ago. I suppose it was his blood pressure that had something to do with it."

"Myron Jettwick's blood pressure?"

"Yes. He'd had a stroke last month and it frightened him tremendously, made him think of death and that sort of thing. Putting his house in order, you know. Of course the Christmas season helped."

Moon never stirred through this, but sat patiently dissecting the jumble and waiting, I knew, for a straight line to emerge. He always worked that way with a gossipy witness, just let him ramble on, which Mr. Spider McRoss certainly did.

"Christmas helped," McRoss chattered on, "in the sense that it crystallized Myron's sudden decision to bring his divorced wife and her stepson out of their banishment and shower them with some seasonal goodwill, while restoring them to his good graces. It was funny, of course."

"What was, Mr. McRoss?"

"It was funny when I found out Helen Jettwick's and Bruce Jettwick's status. I knew something of their history, both from odds and ends that Myron had told me, and from newspaper items that I looked up over at the public library. She'd been a singer of sorts herself, you know, although not nearly as good a one as her son turned out to be. Anyhow, I'd pictured her as eking out the grubbiest sort of existence and probably giving fifty-cent music lessons to the neighborhood brats. That's why I say it was funny to find her installed in a very stunning apartment on the upper east side, and with Bruce hauling down two thousand a week in radio."

"Didn't Myron Jettwick know of that?"

"No, I'm quite certain that he didn't."

"Hadn't he kept in touch with them at all?"

"No."

"Then how did you find them?"

"I found them through Wallace Emberry. Myron was peculiar that way. He wanted his lawyer to keep a casual eye on them, which Emberry did during the past fifteen years, but he forbade Emberry ever to mention their names in his presence. Everybody's a little screwy here or there, don't you think?"

"Fortunately. A world of utter sanity would be a madhouse in itself."

"Of course with a man of Myron's wealth, the word was 'eccentric.'"

"You were the ambassador, then, between Myron Jettwick and his divorced wife and Bruce?"

"Yes. It took several visits, and finally even Emberry had to add his persuasions."

"Just what was your method?"

"A simple one, Mr. Moon. I touched on the frightening stroke from blood pressure and Myron's subsequent desire to effect a reconciliation both with her and with Bruce. Then I painted a general Yuletide softening on the part of Myron's heart with an encompassing wish for peace on earth and goodwill toward all men. Curiously, I believe that Myron was perfectly sincere in that. He seemed to have developed a determination to spray forgiveness and blessings around the landscape with an almost religious fervor. He even started going to church."

"Just what was Helen Jettwick's reaction to all this?"

"Well, after I'd worked on her for a while, and then after Emberry had—both of us were trying to convince her of Myron's genuine sincerity—she broke down. And that was funny, too."

"How?"

"In her way of doing it. When she finally did accept the invitation for this cruise she said that I was to tell Myron that she was 'afraid to refuse.'"

"Where is her apartment?"

"It's on Fifty-sixth Street, just east of Park, one of those nice reconverted houses with an automatic lift and trees on the sidewalk. Number Ten-B."

"What church was it Mr. Jettwick started going to?"

"It's rather a high Episcopalian one. I found it completely incense and intoning. It's in the Chelsea district, over on West Twenty-second Street near the river."

"What was the name of his doctor?"

"Winston, Doctor Arthur B. Winston, on Park."

"Who were his business associates?"

"Myron's? He had none. That was one of the reasons for his great success, if you ask me."

"There seems to have been a double-barreled angle to this proposed Caribbean cruise. On the one hand we have a leisurely opportunity under agreeable circumstances for effecting a reconciliation with his divorced wife and Bruce, and then we have Mrs. Harriet Schuyler. Were Mr. Jettwick and Mrs. Schuyler planning some real-estate merger or deal?"

"Yes, I'm quite sure of it."

"Do you know what it was?"

"No, beyond the fact that I think it concerned Staten Island."

"Even as his confidential secretary, Mr. Jettwick did not confide his business plans to you?"

"As I've said, just to an extent. I'd say that his only complete confidante was his black steel box."

"Good. We needed that."

Spider McRoss smiled quickly.

"The 'missing papers,' Mr. Moon?"

"Yes, with any luck."

"Perhaps there will be. I didn't notice the box beside the bed this morning, when we went in after the alarm."

"It had been there?"

"Yes. Myron always carried it about with him on his trips, and it was there last night when he sent for me about six. It was on the night table by his bed."

Moon could do some leaping about, too.

"Why did he send for you?"

"He wanted me to order flowers for Mrs. Jettwick. He seemed suddenly to have remembered a fondness on her part for Parma violets. I thought it a rather nice touch."

"Describe the box, please, Mr. McRoss."

"Well, black enamel, one of those dispatch things. I'd say about eighteen inches long, by six wide and three deep, with a very good combination lock on it."

"Do the police know about it as yet?"

"No, I don't think so. Should they?"

"Yes."

"Perhaps I'd better go and tell them?"

"Perhaps you had."

I said to Moon, after McRoss had left us to carry his glamorous chit-chat to the cops:

"Just what's the matter with that guy?"

Moon thought for quite a while before he answered, and I suspected that he was going psychic on me. He was, in a way, but I didn't get the full force of it until afterward. Moon said:

"He knows too much."

SIX

THE TAPPING FINGER

A small clock on a false mantel in the library struck four bells.

Moon shut his eyes and had me read back through the notes to date. He says it doesn't do the slightest good, but that it soothes him. It soothes him because my voice, if I could sing, would combine the better features of a train announcer and a synthetic baritone going home on a Negro spiritual of the sort that finds unhappiness in shirts and looks on shoes like strait jackets.

All that is nonsense, because I can tell from a habit Moon has of tapping his forefinger when I come to a point that he wants to remember.

Here's a list of the taps:

Miss Jettwick: "A sailor was clearing the snow—"

Bruce Jettwick: "I'd say maybe three minutes, or five at the most."

Bruce Jettwick: "—and we'd only spoken a few words together last night."

Bruce Jettwick: "He was under the covers—"

Bruce Jettwick: "If I had to stop him from ruining Mother's life again, and mine—"

Miss Jettwick: "—whereas Mrs. Schuyler has been known to plunge her whole fortune blindly—"

McRoss: "She married Myron's younger brother Alfred first."

McRoss: "—and Mrs. Blackman insisted on prosecuting."

McRoss: "—if it hadn't been for Jeffry Smith."

McRoss: "No, I'm quite certain that he didn't."

McRoss: "He even started going to church."

McRoss: "—to tell Myron that she was 'afraid to refuse.'"

McRoss: "—I think it concerned Staten Island."

McRoss: "—by six wide and three deep, with a very good combination lock on it."

The clock struck five bells by the time I was through. Moon asked me to root out the sailor who had discovered the crime, and to bring him back.

I went out on deck and caught a few lungfuls of cold fresh air while watching McRoss lean across the starboard rail and push his face into white stars of photoflash bulbs operated by cameramen on the landing stage below. I saw the results later in the evening editions, where McRoss stared out of front pages, with that zany look, under headings the most typical of which was:

JETTWICK SECRETARY GASPS AFTER GRILLING.

Near him was one of *Trade Wind*'s officers. He was a nice-looking young chap with the beefy skin that comes from constant weather. He turned out to be Talbot, and he told me that the snow-shoveling sailor's name was Johnson and that I'd find him in the crew's quarters forward, either dying or dead.

Johnson was practically both when I got to him. He was stretched flat on his bunk with the sort of a hangover that even Hollywood would be at a loss for a superlative to describe. I asked him if he minded coming back to the library with me and talking with Moon, and he said that if Moon was an undertaker he'd be delighted to, and would give him carte-blanche.

Moon stared, fascinated, at Johnson's glaceed eyes and asked him to sit down.

"I will make this as painless as possible, Mr. Johnson."

"Pain?" Johnson snorted, and wished he hadn't.

"Have you done much snow shoveling?"

"Plenty. I was born in Vermont."

"Did you notice anything about the condition of the snow when you were clearing the aft-deck this morning?

"I didn't notice anything about anything until I saw that stiff. Why worry about snow?"

"You will realize its importance. Try to remember whether the edge of your shovel slid over the decking smoothly, or whether it struck any hard spots."

"Oh, God."

Johnson figuratively took his head in his hands and tried to think.

"Yes, there were some hard spots."

"What condition do you find in snow after a man has walked or stood on it for some time?"

"It packs down. Sometimes, if he stands long enough in one place it gets solid like ice. That's what I need, ice!"

"Shortly, Mr. Johnson. Tell me about the hard spots your shovel struck this morning."

"Say, you're right, brother. They were spaced just about how a man would walk, and there was a hard, icy patch just under the open port-hole."

"Thank you, Mr. Johnson." Moon smiled faintly and added, "Happy New Year."

"That's all right."

Johnson got to the library door before he decided to be insulted.

"A happy New Year, hell!"

District Attorney Seward came in just as Johnson was going out. He glanced at Johnson and then said to Moon:

"Another corpse?"

"Yes."

"If the rest of the crew were in the same condition that he was in last night, anybody could have come aboard and slit throats with impunity. Why the interview?"

Moon told him.

"Do you agree with me, Mr. Seward, that the man or woman who stood in the snow before that open porthole was either the perpetrator or an eyewitness to the crime?"

"Yes, and I'm glad you thought of that angle. I came to tell you that the body is on its way to the city mortuary and that a few reports on the post mortem ought to trickle in this afternoon by around four."

"Care to bet on the bullet?" Moon said.

"Oh, that."

Seward's smile brushed the bullet aside. The smile stayed, and this time it meant something.

I didn't like it. Neither did Moon.

Six bells from the false mantelpiece said it was eleven o'clock.

SEVEN

AN INTEREST IN FLOWERS

Moon finished looking at Seward's smile, and then asked him whether or not McRoss had told him about the black steel box. McRoss had, and some of the ferrets from Center Street were already taking Myron Jettwick's quarters apart in search of it.

The three of us went below and had a look.

The place had cleared out considerably. Chief Medical Examiner Dutton had gone, the photographers and fingerprint boys had finished, and Assistant Police Commissioner McGilvray and his secretary were up in Captain Plummet's quarters wading through the crew.

Only a sergeant of detectives and a plain-clothes man were left, and they were methodically hunting for the black steel box with that official sort of patience which always amazes me. They were testing the wood paneling in the living room when we got there, and so far they had had no luck.

Seward doubted whether the box would be found aboard the yacht. Moon doubted whether it would be found aboard the yacht. I saw no reason for not doubting it also, all of which got us some sour looks from the busy seekers, especially the plain-clothes man who was digging out a splinter from his thumb.

Seward told us that he had to have New Year's dinner with his wife and kids, murder or no murder, and that he'd come back to the yacht around four in the afternoon and question Miss Jettwick, Helen Jettwick, McRoss, and Bruce on board rather than dragging them downtown to his office, which, incidentally, saved him from dragging himself down there, too.

Then he smiled again, which took the place of reminding us that the autopsy reports should start coming in by that time, gave us a bright good-by and left.

I followed Moon into the bedroom. He went over and looked down at the empty bed. One pillowcase had been removed for evidence. It would be the bloodstained one against which Jettwick's head had rested.

Built into the wall within reach of the side of the bed were two shelves for books. Moon made no effort to remove them. The detective sergeant and plain-clothes man would already have done that and have returned them carefully to their proper places.

Moon said:

"Look up Miss Jettwick, will you please, Bert? Ask her whether her brother made a hobby of botany. If she doesn't know, ask Helen Jettwick and McRoss."

I left him staring thoughtfully at about two feet of books with botanical titles that formed a small block in the center of the second shelf, and went up above to the main deck. Seward's smile stayed with me, and I tried to figure what else he expected the autopsy to produce beyond the murder bullet, which was a fine time for young love to come rearing its pretty head. The female section of it was standing at the top of the companionway, still vivid in arsenical green, but otherwise pretty limp.

I wanted to breeze on lightly about my botanical research, but Elizabeth stopped me and said:

"I'm worried, Mr. Stanley. I'm worried very much." It struck me that she had been crying, and being a push-over for tears, in common with the rest of the world's male population, I started a there-there, and she told me please not to there-there her as she was no longer a child, and that people had stopped patting her on the head over ten years ago after she had patted the last well-meaning idiot who had done so right back.

Well, if she wanted to be treated as a contemporary that was all right with me, so I took one foot back out of the grave of my thirty-four years and said:

"I don't blame you, Miss Schuyler. I'm worried, too. What's yours?"

"I think that Mr. Moon ought to be up in the captain's quarters with Bruce. That police commissioner has been questioning him now for twenty minutes, and nobody's with him but Wallace Emberry, and you know him."

"Mr. Emberry is an excellent lawyer."

She quit being limp for a minute.

"Very excellent. Mr. Emberry couldn't be finer for running up a last will and testament over crumpets and tea, but turn him loose against a practical cop on a murder case and he'd even forget when to yell yoicks."

Well, I agreed with her in this completely, but I felt sorry for her very white face. It had one of the most hectic make-up jobs on it I'd seen in years.

"Don't forget one thing, Miss Schuyler, about Emberry. If I remember his record, he started his practice in the criminal courts, and anybody who's once ridden a bicycle doesn't forget how."

It was not one of my happiest comparisons because she cut it up into neat pieces, and then said:

"I know just how desperate the spot is that Bruce is in. Unless Mr. Moon can prove that Mr. Jettwick was dead when Bruce went in there at three o'clock this morning, Bruce is sunk. Can he?"

"Why not take the other point of view? Can the police prove that Mr. Jettwick was alive?"

She gave me one look that was like any tall, iced, acid-base drink, and walked away.

I continued my own route into the main saloon. Miss Jettwick, Helen Jettwick, Harriet Schuyler, and McRoss were all there.

There was a nervous hush about the place, for no one was talking, but they sat huddled in chairs and looking like zombies in the mixed light of a murky saffron from the portholes, and the shallow indirect effect from some ceiling fixtures which were turned on. It was like a funeral, but without any flowers and without any grief, just worry and doubts and fear instead.

They all looked up at me as if they were faced by some perfect stranger who had just crashed interstellar space.

I said:

"Miss Jettwick, was your brother interested in botany? Did he make a hobby of it? Mr. Moon wants to know."

"Myron? I don't think so, Mr. Stanley. I only saw him infrequently for a great many years, just when I'd come East from the coast, but I'm certain he never showed any interest in flowers."

"How about it, Mrs. Jettwick? Back in the days when you were married to him, did he show any interest them?'"

"None, none whatever, Mr. Stanley." She added bitterly. "He was a dilettante in little beyond roast beef."

For a moment this stopped me, there was so much honed steel in it, while it seemed almost reasonable to picture Helen Jettwick pulling a gun and pumping a bullet into a head she'd just been chatting with.

Then I turned to McRoss who was running white fingers over the crests of his slick dark locks.

"You've been closer to him than anybody recently, Mr. McRoss. How about it?"

"Flowers? Myron and flowers? Dear, no. I mean, I'd say the subject not only would have bored him, but he'd have utterly ignored it."

Harriet Schuyler, who wasn't on the list for questioning, made the most sense of any of them.

"Might I suggest," she said, taking the chair, "that botany, landscape gardening and kindred subjects might prove an almost essential study for any man involved in real estate and the development of large tracts? Forgive my natural curiosity, Mr. Stanley, but just why does Mr. Moon want to know?"

I said I didn't know, because I really didn't know, and went down again and joined Moon in the bedroom. He was not exactly in a trance, but he answered me absently when I gave him a digest of my botanical findings and asked him what he had wanted them for.

"Those books, Bert." This, in his absent voice. I always expect, when he uses it, to see Protoplasm Mary swim down through the ceiling and slap me with a wet rubber glove. "That block is entirely on botany. It is long enough to cover an eighteen-inch steel box and there is enough space behind them for its depth. I believe Jettwick kept the box there, feeling it would not be disturbed as botanical books are not the type a person would pick out if looking for something to read."

"Well, well," I said, trying to snap him out of it. "So whoever stole the box must have wondered why Jettwick kept books on botany and become suspicious like you."

Moon was still far, far away.

"Yes."

"What's bothering you? Why do this to me?"

"This is bothering me, Bert."

Moon opened his right hand. Lying on the palm of it was a fragment of nutshell. It was smooth, and its color was a heavy amber brown.

"Sapucaia?"

"Yes."

"Well, what? Bruce and you have both admitted that he was in here last night."

"Doing certain things, Bert, yes. But not eating nuts. It disturbs me. It shows leisure, conversation, a calculating pause. You do not start eating nuts when shocked into sudden contemplation of a corpse.

"I'm beginning to wonder whether that was why Seward smiled."

As we were soon to know, it was and it wasn't. The reason why it really wasn't is because it was worse.

"Where did you find it?"

"On the floor, just behind that leg at the foot of the bed."

"Standing there, eating nuts and dropping shells."

"That's right."

Moon vanished deeper still.

EIGHT

THE EVIDENCE OF A NUT

Seward came back to *Trade Wind* shortly before four. He looked formal, very polite, and his eyes were perfectly cold. In fact he couldn't have looked more sinister if he'd had a warrant for arrest clasped in his hand.

His secretary was with him. The secretary's name was Mort Wilbur. He was a neat little trick, complete with pince-nez, and as unobtrusive as something barely visible in a fog.

The interim had been peaceful, because Moon had decided to go back to *Coquilla* for lunch. We'd finished this by two, and Moon had then taken his regular hour's sleep after the midday meal. He never misses this except from some disaster of the nature that insurance companies label an act of God.

We had just finished greeting Miss Jettwick in *Trade Wind*'s main saloon when Seward, plus Wilbur, came in.

Seward said, after his own greetings and introducing Wilbur and all that:

"I wonder whether I might turn the library into an office for this afternoon, Miss Jettwick?"

"Certainly, Mr. Seward."

"Could I also bother you to send word to your nephew, and ask him to join me there?"

"Of course, but I thought Commissioner McGilvray had already taken Bruce's statement?"

Seward smiled, very cold, very correct.

"The police department and the district attorney's office frequently pursue independent lines of investigation, Miss Jettwick."

"I see."

Seward turned to Moon.

"Do you and Mr. Stanley wish to be with us?"

"Thank you, Mr. Seward. Yes."

Well, there was Emily Post all over the place and things were just too *soigné* for words, and the four of us beat it for the library where Wilbur copped a seat before the desk and laid out a limp-leather loose-leaf notebook and six pencils sharpened into needles.

Moon hoped that Seward had enjoyed his festive New Year's meal with Mrs. Seward and the two little Sewards, and Seward admitted pleasantly that he had, and said that the turkey had weighed eighteen pounds, stuffed with chestnuts and oysters, and that the two kids had each weighed a hundred pounds by the time that the mince pie and hard sauce had come along and were now blissfully in the arms of indigestion.

Then Bruce came in.

Bruce looked about the way you'd expect any youngster to look who'd been up all night going through hell and was being forced to face one of the smartest prosecuting officials that had ever held office.

Seward asked him to sit down.

"Mr. Jettwick," Seward said, "I must warn you that my secretary will take your statement down in shorthand. It will later be transcribed and I shall ask you to sign it. It is your privilege to refuse to do so, inasmuch as you have not been charged with any crime. I suggest, however, that you waive that privilege."

"Certainly I'll waive it," Bruce said. "I told everything to Mr. McGilvray, and I can only repeat it to you."

"Thank you. As Mr. Emberry undoubtedly instructed you, a statement is of small practical value in a trial court unless it is backed up by tangible circumstantial evidence or corroborated by an eyewitness. I have no desire to trap you, Mr. Jettwick, so I will admit freely that evidence has been brought to my attention which convinces me that your uncle was still alive when you went back to see him in his quarters at three o'clock this morning. I cannot be fairer than that."

There was no movement from Moon. I knew he had been expecting something like this.

Bruce hadn't. Bruce had a set of good, honest, dark brown eyes, and they suddenly looked more than just dead tired. They looked sick.

"I'm sorry, Mr. Seward, but you're mistaken. My uncle was dead."

"I advise that you reconsider."

"I can't reconsider, Mr. Seward. He was dead. His breath would have shown on the mirror if he hadn't been."

Moon said to Seward:

"Forgive me, but you're not leading up to any cataleptic trance condition, are you?"

"No, it's nothing obscure, nothing like that. Mr. Jettwick, please go back to the point yesterday when you and your mother came aboard the yacht. You did arrive together?"

"Yes, we got here shortly after six."

"What luggage had you? Just yours, not your mother's."

"I had two wardrobe suitcases, and a small case fitted with toilet articles, and a hatbox."

"Were they all locked when they were brought on board?"

"Yes."

"Were they taken directly to your cabin?"

"Yes. Mr. McRoss greeted us. He suggested that Mother and I go down to our cabins and unpack, and then join my uncle and the rest for cocktails in the main saloon in about an hour. A steward brought my bags down with me, and left them in the cabin."

"Did he unpack them or did you?"

"No, he offered to, but I said I preferred doing it myself."

"Be patient with me, please, if I seem to harp on precise detail. Were the bags still locked when the steward left the cabin?"

"Yes, Mr. Seward. I unlocked them, put my things away, and then put the bags in a cupboard. I showered, dressed, called at Mother's cabin for her, and we went up to the main saloon."

"Please, a lot more detail, Mr. Jettwick. You put the bags in a cupboard. Did you lock them before doing so?"

"I locked the small one, yes, but not the other two."

"Did you lock the small one because of the opened box of revolver cartridges you had left in it?"

"Yes. There seemed no point in having the room steward come across them and start talking."

"You had previously removed enough of them to load your gun?"

"Yes, that's right."

"We shan't bother with your reasons for carrying a gun on a friendly cruise aboard the yacht of a close relative, Mr. Jettwick. That is an angle which I will develop later. Right now I'm interested in the locked suitcase. The opened box of cartridges was in it when you put it away in the cupboard. What else?"

"Just a can of nuts, Mr. Seward."

"Ah, yes. We must consider that can of nuts."

"They're sapucaias. I got to like them when I was a kid, during one winter that Mother sang down in Rio de Janeiro with some ghastly musical-comedy troupe. You can't get them up here. A friend sends them up to me. He sent that can as a present for Christmas."

"Let us follow that can from the moment when you came on board. Was it then locked in the small suitcase?"

"Yes."

"So we have it under lock until you unpacked your things in your cabin."

"That's right, Mr. Seward."

"Did you take it out of the suitcase?"

"No. I guess I'm selfish about sapucaias. I figured the room steward might develop a taste for them, too, so I thought they might as well stay locked up."

"Did you eat any of them before doing so?"

"No. I did take some out and stuck them in a pocket, just to have."

"In what pocket, Mr. Jettwick?"

"In my pants pocket."

"Of your dinner clothes?"

"Yes."

"Let this be quite plain, please. We now have some sapucaias in your pocket, and the rest are in the can in a suitcase which is locked, and in the cupboard. Is that right?"

"Yes, Mr. Seward."

"That suitcase is fastened by a combination-lock type of an expensive make. Does anyone other than yourself know the combination?"

"No, nobody's ever wanted to."

Seward turned to Moon. There was no smile. His face was deadly serious and reminded you of the set look that a shepherd dog has on the trail.

"When it was examined this morning, Mr. Moon, the lock showed no sign of having been forced or tampered with. It took the department expert forty minutes to open it up."

"Why on earth didn't he ask me for the combination?" Bruce said.

"The department prefers its little mysteries, Mr. Jettwick. Personally, I have found such tactics a hindrance and believe that a straight line is still the shortest distance between two points. All right now, we have you with the sapucaias in your pocket and going up to the main saloon with your mother. Did you offer a sapucaia to anyone during the evening?"

"No."

"Are you positive of that?"

"Quite positive."

"Could anybody have taken one from you without your knowledge?"

"Scarcely, unless I'd been unconscious, and I definitely wasn't unconscious."

"Did you eat one yourself?"

"No."

It began to hit me around then that here was a lot of pretty big to-do about some bits of shell. I looked at Moon and caught him in his Goya pose, the kind you see up at the Hispanic Museum, very don-somebody and reserved and looking straight down his nose. It was bad. It meant that he suspected a trap, too, and was worried as all hell.

Seward went straight-lining on, and concealing beautifully the Einstein twist.

"Mr. Jettwick, I understand from your statement to Commissioner McGilvray that the New Year's Eve celebration in the main saloon broke up shortly after one in the morning and that you then went directly down to your cabin."

"Yes, Mr. Seward."

"Were you then alone in your cabin?"

"Yes."

"Did you bolt its door?"

"Yes."

"Were the sapucaias still in your pocket?"

"Yes."

"Repeat, please, your movements after you had bolted your cabin door."

"Just how detailed do you want this, Mr. Seward?"

"Pretty much."

"Well, I took my coat off. Then I got a book and lay down on top of the bed and tried to read. I couldn't read. I was thinking, or trying to, about too many things. Shall I go into them?"

"No, not now. You removed nothing but your coat?"

"Nothing."

"Did you sleep at all?"

"Not sleep, really. I was too nervous for that. I must have dozed for a while, because when the boat telephone rang it gave me quite a start. I say dozing, because the bell has a soft tone and I don't think I'd have heard it if I'd been sound asleep."

Moon stirred faintly. Bruce had told us on *Coquilla* that he had finished smoking a cigarette after he had answered the telephone, and that the cigarette had been about half smoked at the moment when the bell rang. That didn't gibe in anybody's language with this new slant that the bell had jerked Bruce out of a doze.

Then Moon lapsed into a quiet blank again and I went back to spasmodic pothooks, while envying Mouse Wilbur whose pencil flew over his loose-leaf notebook with a streamlined ease.

"All right," Seward said. "You answered the telephone and then what?"

"Well, I finished smoking a cigarette."

Seward's head jerked up, and it was a cinch that the slip was in the bag. Bruce must have caught the jerk because he flushed a deep beet red and stopped looking at Seward and looked over at Moon.

"The cigarette was burning on an ash tray beside the bed, Mr. Moon. I guess that's another sign that I just must have been dozing."

It was a neat recovery, and Moon came to bat and smiled reassuringly.

"Certainly it is, and an excellent one, too. It's stupid to suppose that you could recall the length of the ash?"

"Gosh, no, I don't remember that."

"It's inconsequential," Seward said, without meaning it, and then added, "Again from your statement to Commissioner McGilvray, you finished the cigarette before starting for your uncle's quarters?"

"Yes, Mr. Seward."

"You were still completely dressed except for your coat?"

"Yes. I put the coat on before leaving the cabin."

"The sapucaias were still in your trouser pocket?"

"They must have been, Mr. Seward. I hadn't taken them out."

"This question is simply for the record. I realize its improbability, but I want it down. Could anyone have entered your cabin while you were alternately dozing and worrying, and have removed a sapucaia from your trouser pocket?"

"Of course not. The door was still bolted, Mr. Seward."

Again Seward turned to Moon.

"As you've probably determined, the bolt is of a type that cannot conceivably be unfastened from the outside."

"I haven't," Moon said pleasantly, "but I'm convinced, if you say so, of the fact."

"Now then, Mr. Jettwick, you unbolted your door, went aft along the passageway, and knocked on the door of your uncle's quarters. You met or saw nobody in the passageway?"

"Nobody."

"You received no reply to your knock. You found the door unlocked. You entered your uncle's quarters. Right?"

"Sure it's right, Mr. Seward."

"Were you familiar with them?"

"No, I'd never been in them before."

"I suggest at this point, Mr. Jettwick, that you forget the statement which you gave to Commissioner McGilvray, and tell me what occurred.

I suggest this most strongly for your own sake. I am a reasonable man and, frankly, would prefer to like you and believe you. But I insist on truth."

"I did tell the truth, the absolute truth, Mr. Seward."

Seward hardened and became politer than ever.

"Then repeat it, please, from the point when you entered your uncle's living room."

"The lights were on, and it was empty. I saw an open door, and went to it. It was the bedroom, and my uncle was sitting up in the bed, shot."

"You are satisfied that the living room was empty and, except for your uncle, the bedroom was empty?"

"Perfectly satisfied."

"Are you also satisfied that nobody other than yourself and your uncle were in, or entered, those rooms while you were in them?"

"Yes."

"What did you say to your uncle?"

"Nothing, Mr. Seward. He was dead."

"What did he say to your"

"Nothing—my God, Mr. Seward, I tell you he was dead."

"Did he remain in the bed, or did he walk around while both of you were talking?"

"I tell you, I swear, I—Please, Mr. Seward, don't go on like that. My uncle was dead."

"Very well. We have your word, then, that your uncle said nothing, and made no physical movement whatever of his own volition while you were in his presence?"

"You've my word, yes, and anything you like. Don't they swear things like that on a Bible? I'm not being sacrilegious. I'll do it. I'll swear it on a Bible if that will help convince you."

"Just your statement is sufficient, thank you, for our needs."

Moon didn't like that "for our needs" crack one bit. He tried to force Seward's hand.

He said:

"I cannot help feeling that there is an emphasis on sapucaias in your line of questioning. I admit that for a while they bothered me, too. I refer to a fragment of sapucaia shell which I found on the floor at the foot of the bed in Mr. Myron Jettwick's quarters. As I remarked at the time to Mr. Stanley, the presumption that my client had stood there and cracked and eaten a nut might show a debatable mood of contemplation while regarding the corpse of his uncle. On the other hand, under the mental shock and horror of suddenly viewing a death by violence, the act of eating a nut undoubtedly was done subconsciously and completely forgotten. Such, I feel certain, was the case."

"But I didn't eat a nut," Bruce said. "I'll admit that I felt pretty knocked out, but I don't think I drew a blank, and I don't remember eating any nut."

"Do you remember every cigarette you've ever smoked?" Moon asked.

"No, certainly not."

"Well, both acts are comparable, in the sense that either could be done absently as with any habit. I again stress the emotional shock that had gripped you, Mr. Jettwick."

"You—you've got me going, Mr. Moon. Maybe—I don't know—it *is* the sort of thing you could do without knowing it."

"Am I now to understand," Seward said, much too patiently, "that you admit to a possibility, Mr. Jettwick, of having stood at the foot of your uncle's bed, and having cracked and eaten a sapucaia?"

"Mr. Seward, yes. If there was a shell there it must be a possibility, but I don't remember it."

"I think that covers everything. In digest what you state is this: to your admitted knowledge, no sapucaia nut left your possession from the time you boarded the yacht until you were satisfied that your uncle was dead. Do you consider that a fair summary?"

"Perfectly fair, Mr. Seward."

"Then I shall ask you to sign it, after Mr. Wilbur's notes have been transcribed."

Things loosened up on the surface during the quarter of an hour that it took Nimble Wilbur to type out an original and two carbons of his notes. But only on the surface. Seward still had that shepherd-dog look, and Moon stayed Goya.

Bruce, poor kid, was the only one who seemed relieved. He was so relieved, in fact, that he leaned back in his chair and fell sound asleep.

Moon brought up the subject of the autopsy returns, if any, and Seward became suspiciously frank and obliging. He said that a comparison test had been made between the murder bullet taken from Myron Jettwick's skull and a bullet fired from Bruce's gun. The bullets were totally dissimilar, and so Bruce's registered gun was not the murder gun.

On the other hand, Seward pointed out with the good old Seward charm, the East River was a swift deep river, and the actual murder gun could simply have been tossed into it right after the crime. It could even have been tossed into it straight through the open porthole near Myron Jettwick's bed.

Obviously, Seward held a cavalier attitude toward guns, and was willing to discuss them inside and out until the cows came home. And he did do just that until Wilbur whipped the last sheets from the machine and arranged the original and carbons in three very neat piles and then stapled them with fasteners along each top.

Seward woke Bruce up. He made him read a copy carefully and completely straight through. He asked Bruce to sign. Bruce did. Seward asked Moon and me to witness the signature. We did.

Then Seward fired his blast.

"Mr. Jettwick," he said, "you are probably not familiar with the ordinary routine of a post mortem. One aspect of that routine is of vital concern to the situation in which you now stand. I warned you at the outset that evidence had been brought to my attention which convinced me that your uncle was still alive when you went back to see him in his quarters at three o'clock this morning. I am now confident that that evidence, when taken in conjunction with the statement you have just made, and signed under no compulsion or threat, will also convince a jury. For Mr. Moon's sake, I will give you that evidence at once."

It was so quiet that you could have heard even Wilbur drop.

"One of the routine procedures in a post mortem," Seward went on, "is to list the stomach contents and the intestinal contents of the body. You must understand that during the early stages of digestion gross particles of masticated food are retained in the stomach, until they are later changed into chyme, which gradually empties into the duodenum from the stomach. Naturally, Mr. Jettwick, those gross particles retain their characteristics, and are identifiable."

Seward let that sink before he went on.

"Unhappily for you, Mr. Jettwick, the medical examiner found in your uncle's stomach some particles of sapucaia nut which had been swallowed immediately prior to your uncle's death. I have your own clear admission that you alone were in possession of this rare type of nut. I am forced to conclude that you offered your uncle one, and that he accepted it, and swallowed it, immediately before you shot him. *Dead men do not eat*!"

I prefer to draw the veil. Seward said, of course, that Bruce would be taken down to the Tombs and detained for investigation, which was a polite way of saying he'd be kept in a cage until the grand jury handed down an indictment charging him with murder in the first degree.

Moon stood up. He faces jolts that way. He seemed to stretch, even taller than he naturally is, as if he needed every inch of stature in him. His response to that second-act curtain of Seward's put more heart back into young Bruce than any long-winded speech of reassurance could possibly have done.

Moon looked directly at Seward and simply said, with none of that reverence which any reference to one-celled fruits with hardened pericarps always brings into his voice:

"Nuts."

NINE

"BRING YOUR GUN"

The next hour was a mess. It always is, the one which immediately follows an arrest. Moon never endures it. He has a habit of gracefully retiring and letting me be the wailing wall, claiming that my bartender days have hardened me into a state of insensibility to all and sundry grief. He says it depresses him to a point where he loses his valuable ability to think clearly and with effect.

When he pulls that one I always pass.

He left *Trade Wind*, so that he could think clearly and with effect, and did not go back to *Coquilla* where we could have snagged him, but taxied over to the men's bar in the Plaza and fought off being depressed with the assistance of Irish whisky and plain water.

In the meanwhile the bag was mine. The reactions to Bruce's arrest were important and had to be collected, because I knew that Moon would want them after he decided to stop being sheltered and came back to work.

The good-by, good-by scene took place in the main saloon and it couldn't have been drearier. It was about a quarter past five, and the bunch were going through some mechanical motions of being a well-bred group of pukkah sahibs wading through their regular afternoon tea. Even the snow was still falling.

Seward was very decent about it.

He went directly over to Helen Jettwick and said to her:

"I'm sorry to have bad news for you, Mrs. Jettwick. We are detaining your son for investigation. He will be perfectly comfortable and well cared for. I suggest that you disabuse your mind of the average person's conception of such detention. I refer to rubber hoses and the paraphernalia usually attributed to third degrees. Both Mr. Emberry and Mr. Moon will have my permission to confer with him at any time they care to do so. I sincerely hope that one or both of them will succeed in convincing me that I have made a mistake. I will be equally sincere in telling you that I do not believe I have."

"Where is he? May I see him?"

"Certainly, Mrs. Jettwick. He is in the library."

I'd rather not remember the way Helen Jettwick found the door and left the main saloon. There's a certain fumbling that it hurts too much to look at.

Old-England Emberry disentangled himself from buttered crumpets and oolong, and bore down on Seward in a faint cloud of lavender scent which drifted from cartographic tweeds and his apple-polished skin. I expected him to say: "Preposterous."

He said, "Preposterous!" Then he hooked Seward by an arm and gusted him out of the main saloon on an added:

"I'll have a writ of *habeas corpus* as soon as I can get in touch with Judge Broderick. I shall demand bail. We'll meet it to any figure, Seward—any!"

They left, with Emberry still demanding, and then was the first good opportunity I had for taking in Mrs. Schuyler and young Elizabeth.

Mrs. Schuyler first. You couldn't miss it, the way she was trying not to look smug. Even in spite of her my-dear-this-is-too-too-silly-but-isn't-it-ghastly attitude you couldn't miss it. She was wearing a black broadcloth afternoon number reminiscent of the heyday of Worth, and had a dog collar of black opals around her throat that must have cost a junior fortune.

She moved in on Emma Jettwick, who was sitting on a settee and had taken everything like a brick, clutched one of Miss Jettwick's hands and said, "There's nothing I can say, my dear—nothing!"

So she went right on and talked for the next five minutes, which gave me time to shift to Elizabeth. I'd expected her to be on the verge of a nervous collapse, but had forgotten the red hair. She'd stopped being elegant with a Minton cup and had gone over to a cellaret and mixed herself a good hooker of scotch. I took it out of her hand and said, "Thanks. Sherry for you, Miss Schuyler."

"Just what's the idea of that, Mr. Stanley?"

I tried to save my life by admitting to her that a careworn debutante could easily drink a retired bartender under a table, but pointed out that right now there was no place for a table. As well be King Canute and shake a finger at the sea. She said, "Oh?" and took the glass back, and probably would have found herself in a fine stupor if her mother hadn't stopped for breath and said, "Elizabeth, is that a highball?"

"Yes, Mother."

"Pour yourself a glass of sherry, dear, and give that thing to me."

"Yes, Mother."

My opinion of exclusive finishing schools went up a peg when I caught the restraint it must have cost Elizabeth to walk sedately over, hand the glass to her mother, come back, and pour out some sherry, before rocking me on my heels with an underbreath damn.

Spider McRoss was the last specimen for the slide. He had been standing at a porthole looking out across the deck to the landing stage. His villainous eyebrows were tight in a straight line, and, although I've only hearsay knowledge of a hawk's gaze, his had it bad. He moved alongside us and said, "You know how these things go, Mr. Stanley. I mean now that they've taken Bruce, how about the rest of us?"

A good deal of chichi had gone out of his voice and he sounded pretty tense, and as though he wanted a straight answer.

"So far as the rest of you are concerned, Mr. McRoss, the fact that Mr. Jettwick is being detained for investigation doesn't mean a thing. The fact that Seward is certain he has an open-and-shut case doesn't mean a thing. What does mean something is that Mr. Moon believes in young Jettwick's innocence."

"Of course, naturally, we all of us do, but I'm not referring to that. Neither Commissioner McGilvray nor District Attorney Seward said anything definite about our, well, freedom of movement."

"There's nothing they can say, unless they want to detain you the way they're detaining Mr. Jettwick."

"But suppose you wanted to leave town?"

"Then they'd probably detain you."

"There's a policeman still standing at the head of the gangway. Would he stop you if you wanted to leave the yacht?"

"No."

"What's he there for, then?"

"Probably to save Miss Jettwick from annoyance from the press, from curiosity seekers."

"You mean I could just walk ashore and nothing would happen?"

"No, I don't mean that. You'd be tailed."

"Really? Well!"

Elizabeth said, "Then Mother and I could go home?"

"I'm quite sure of it. Will you?"

She looked over at her mother, and there was something I couldn't get in her expression, but it wasn't right. She said, "I don't know."

Then you did get it, suddenly, from the way her eyes were opened wider than normal and a tightness about her mouth. It was fear. I suppose working with Moon had hardened me to murder in the sense that you came to look upon it as a game, the who-did-it, and the why-and-how being more important than any personal element involved. It must be the same way with men whose business is poisonous snakes, getting callous to them through habit, the way we were callous about the chance that the person right at your elbow throughout an investigation might be the guy who committed the crime.

Well, Elizabeth had had no chance during her seventeen years to get callous. You could almost see the way her thoughts were running: there he was (Myron Jettwick) moving, talking, breathing, enjoying, and suffering the business of living, sitting up in his bed and surrounded by the security of his own familiar things, certainly familiar enough with his murderer to lean back against the pillows and chat, then startlingly to face that deadly change. The change of face, from someone whom you know, into the face of Death.

From someone whom you know.

There was the crux of it so far as Elizabeth was concerned. I didn't believe for a minute that even a hardened debutante could seriously picture her own mother pumping lead into flesh and wiping out a human life, but the nasty fact remained that Harriet Schuyler had been up and dressed at half past six in the morning and had been wearing her hat.

Then again, why had she accepted this proposed cruise in the first place, having practically just brought Elizabeth out, suddenly to snatch her away? It must have meant the cancellation of numberless important dates, a complete disruption of the girl's most imperative social season. It must have been a desperately important reason to have made Harriet Schuyler do that.

It was a relief to get a message from Moon.

A steward brought it in. It was a telegram which Moon had sent from the men's bar at the Plaza, telling me to get in touch with Jimmy Singer. Jimmy runs one of the few reliable private detective agencies in town and Moon always uses him when he needs detailed research work or added men on his cases.

Moon wanted Jimmy to trace the record of two people during the past fifteen years, and to find out the present whereabouts of each. One was the wife of Senator Blackman, the woman who had insisted on prosecuting Helen Jettwick for the jewel theft on *Leviathan*. The other was the correspondent in the ensuing divorce, Mr. Jeffry Smith.

Moon also asked me to arrange with Miss Jettwick that he and I occupy Myron Jettwick's quarters aboard *Trade Wind* for the next few days. He listed the things he wanted moved over from *Coquilla*. Apart from an essential wardrobe and toilet accessories he wanted his copy of Richard Hughes' *A High Wind in Jamaica*, which he reread at least once a year, and a box of Moreton Bay chestnuts which had recently been shipped him from Australia.

He specified only one thing so far as my own stuff was concerned. He told me to bring my gun.

TEN

THROUGH A PORTHOLE

Harriet Schuyler made no move. No one did. They decided to stay on *Trade Wind* even though there was no longer any question (right then) of making the Caribbean cruise.

You could understand McRoss staying. Miss Jettwick had asked him to, and to remain with her and work with Wallace Emberry until her brother's estate could be wound up and put in shape. And you could understand Helen Jettwick staying, rather than suffer the emptiness left in their apartment by Bruce's present sojourn at the Tombs. But Mrs. Schuyler's excuse for subjecting Elizabeth to an environment still foggy with murder was as thin as her reason for her hat.

Her own home was a substantial and expensive house on Madison Avenue that had been in the family for three generations. Elizabeth told me about it with that frankness which, for the young of my day, would have produced some good wallops with the back of a hairbrush and no supper before bed.

I gathered, with no bother at all, that Mrs. Schuyler camouflaged her sharp interest in business by an outward absorption in the world of art, and that her drawing-room was a free-lunch counter for handsome young artistic things who were always on the brink of "arriving," but never did. You ended up by picturing Mrs. Schuyler as a culinary Major Bowes.

Anyhow, Mrs. Schuyler decided to remain for a while on the yacht to escape (the excuse) the sympathetic weaseling of friends which would be more difficult to ward off in her home, unless she declared a state of siege. Later, when the investigation was settled in one way or the other, she said she would take Elizabeth abroad and give her a season both on the Continent and in England.

I didn't believe it for a minute, and neither did Moon when I told him about it after he had decided it was psychologically safe to return from his monastic retreat in the Plaza. This was around eight. Our stuff was by then aboard *Trade Wind* and he asked me, while we dressed for dinner, to arrange for three interviews after the meal. He wanted to see the night watchman who had been on duty last night on the landing stage of Wharf House, also the sailor on deck watch on *Trade Wind* between midnight and four, and Captain Plummet.

It was a gloomy meal, but nobody skipped it. Even Emberry was there to do a little spade work on the estate with Miss Jettwick after coffee.

The cook was almost as fervent an artist as Walter and drew together, among various accessories, a very fine mess of Buzzards Bay oysters, clear green turtle soup, a roast saddle of mutton, plus Château Mouton Rothschild, and a baked Alaska.

I wondered at the ice cream until Elizabeth, who had pecked at mutton, dove overboard into it with no shame at all, and then you appreciated more than ever Miss Jettwick's sound judgment and goodness of heart.

I rounded up Captain Plummet first, gave him Moon's compliments and the request that he join Moon in the owner's quarters. The captain looked no more like what a typical sea captain is supposed to look like than any captain does. He hit the average which, without the uniform, would have made you put him down as a middle-aged, middle-class, moderately successful businessman who knows his job thoroughly but is in constant dread, through some malignant and unpredictable prank of fate, of losing it.

He gave concisely the information Moon wanted. He explained that everything had been a little out-of-the-ordinary last night because of it having been New Year's Eve. The owner had given permission for all men to go ashore and celebrate with their families and friends, with the exception of those required for service in the galley and the steward's department. He said that no watch had been kept until midnight when Terrence, one of the stewards, had been posted on deck to stay there until six.

Moon asked baldly if Terrence had been drunk, and Captain Plummet said equally baldly that Terrence had.

"He had been drinking during the evening, Mr. Moon, and had a pretty good load on even by the time he went on watch. I know that under the circumstances you want the absolute facts, so I'm giving them to you."

Plummet made it unnecessary for Moon to see the night watchman on Wharf House's landing stage by letting us know that the man had spent his tour in a beautiful stupor from nips thrust upon him by tenants and guests either coming or departing for revels which must have been normally wet.

It began to look as though the whole town could have walked aboard *Trade Wind* with nothing to check them but a bleary smile, but Terrence's tale changed that.

I got Terrence after Captain Plummet had left. He was a constitutionally thin young man with sandy hair and a now-you-see-it-now-you-don't mustache. He had the utter assurance of the Irish, and unburdened himself to Moon with the abandon of an Abbey player going to town on his Synge.

He had felt a native irritation that he should have had to work while the majority of the crew were enjoying themselves ashore. He had felt this in spite of the generous bonus which Myron Jettwick had given to those who had stayed on the yacht.

He made us vividly see himself up there on deck in the cold wind and snow, harking to the happy noises of a city engaged in revelry, and feeling very sorry for himself in consequence.

He had passed most of his time near the gangplank, leaning on the rail, and watching the different parties of people arriving at Wharf House. They were people in high good humor, and both *Trade Wind* and *Coquilla* had been targets for their interest. Terrence had talked with several, and had gone down the gangplank and taken a sup from anyone who offered him a flask. You can imagine that the mixtures awash inside of him must have been amazing.

By two o'clock he was halfway down to Rio, and said he had no accurate knowledge of what the man looked like who had given him an opened bottle of Jamaica rum.

"Were you on deck or on the landing stage, Mr. Terrence, when this bottle was given you?"

"I'd swear on my oath, sir, it was the landing stage—but you know."

"Did the man approach you from the yacht or from the direction of Wharf House?"

"Now that I couldn't tell you, Mr. Moon. The way I was feeling then, he might have come from both."

Two facts were significant. Terrence did recall a lot of white shirt front, which suggested that the man had not been wearing an overcoat, and the second fact blasted any hope that some passing stranger had dropped aboard and shot Myron Jettwick for a whim. Terrence hadn't been able to finish the bottle of rum so he had taken it below to his bunk and stowed it, and himself alongside of it, letting any further guarding of *Trade Wind* for the night go bang.

He had found himself face to face with the bottle when he woke up this morning, and he recognized the rum as a special brand with which the yacht was stocked. He hadn't wanted to be accused of stealing from the yacht's stores and had thrown the bottle into the river through a port-hole and that, so help him, was that.

It was plenty.

Moon filed it, then dismissed it from his mind, dismissed Terrence from the living room, and prepared for bed. This involved, while he showered and got into flannel pajamas, sending to the galley for three pâté sandwiches, a pint of milk, and a pear, then fitting them on the bed table along with the box of Moreton Bay chestnuts, Hughes' *A High Wind in Jamaica*, a thermos of ice water, a glass, cigarettes, matches, an ash tray, and a chart for how to find what.

He opened the same porthole that had been opened last night when Myron Jettwick got his, got into bed, said good night, and asked me to close the door.

This left me with the living room to rattle around in, and a cot which the steward had set up in one corner for my frame. There were plenty of blankets, however, so it didn't look too desperate.

I opened a porthole beside it and took some deep breaths of the cold night air. The small aft-deck which arched around the bedroom did not extend this far so when you poked your head out of the porthole you looked straight down on the water, which was about six feet below, very oily, swift and deadly black, and just as cheery as an accomplished ghost.

I got undressed, shoved my gun under the pillow, turned out the lights, went to bed, and slept until the knocking noise woke me up at half past three. Well, you know how it is when something unusual wakes you out of a dead sleep, or if you don't know, you're lucky. It wasn't very loud, but it was a steady bumping sound and came in through the open porthole. I looked from habit at the radium dial of my wrist watch (where-were-you-at-three-thirty-when-etc.) and pulled the gun from under the pillow.

Moon gave me a lecture in the morning on the fundamental laws of physics after he found out what had happened. But, like most lectures, of course, it came too late. My perfectly rational explanation of the dilemma cut no ice with him at all; I mean the fact that if I poked the gun out of the porthole there was no room left for my head, so I couldn't see what to shoot at, and if I poked my head out it became physically impossible also to poke out the gun. Portholes just happen to be that way, that's all.

I chose my head. What with still being half asleep and so forth I couldn't imagine what they were doing. There were two men in a row-boat. It was snowing again in slow fat flakes and that, with the pitch dark of the night, made them look like a couple of vague blots. The boat was some distance forward, and rode jerkily on the swift tide rip of the water. Its rise and fall and swinging were responsible for the bumping noise.

Both of the men were crouched in the bow, and one of them seemed to be holding a rope.

Moon has always been very nice about it, but I know that he thinks I rated a one-way ticket to Bloomingdale for having opened my trap and shouted at them:

"What do you think you're doing?"

Both of them looked up, and the one holding the rope dropped it in his fright. The other man stood up, which brought his head just below the level of my own. He took off a pair of heavy mittens and fumbled with one hand beneath his reefer while fending the rowboat from the yacht's side with the other, as the current carried the boat down toward the porthole and dumb me. Both men wore caps, and the large collars of their reefers covered their chins.

Several things happened simultaneously. I realized that the man had taken his mittens off so his fingers could close around the butt of a gun under his reefer. The tide carried him to a point just alongside of me as he did get his gun out from under his reefer. I poked my own gun through the porthole only to find that because of my head already being through it the only thing I could aim at was Venus.

I know now that if he'd had his silencer along the man would have shot me. As it was, he had to restrain himself and simply belt me one with the butt of his gun on the head. Just before everything went black, as the old saying goes, I did hear the other pirate say:

"Christ, but you shouldn't of done that."

ELEVEN

PLANS FOR TWO-THIRTY

I agreed with him next morning thoroughly. It was seven o'clock before my skull recovered consciousness and a conviction that it had been split open in two parts. The body also took some time to thaw out from the cold blasts that had hit it from the open porthole with nothing to make them hesitate but a pair of magenta-striped silk pajamas Moon had given me for Christmas and which I had always admired until then.

Moon heard me in the bathroom and called to me to come in. I finished washing away dried blood, swabbing the cut with iodine, and plastering an antiseptic pad across a lump the size of a duck egg before doing so. Moon hates to be frightened at any time, but especially right after he wakes up in the morning.

"I had an idea," he said after one look, "that something would happen if we stayed aboard here. I'm glad that we're not disappointed."

He told me to have some melon, a mushroom omelet, and coffee and rolls sent in, and that he'd hear the details of the battle while we ate. Then he shaved, bathed, murdered Rodolfo's narrative from *La Bohème*, and dressed, while I received the steward bearing our breakfast in the living room, and explained my clinical appearance by giving him the stock excuse that my skull had hit an open door in the dark. His answer was very stock, too.

Moon chased the steward and said we'd serve ourselves. He finished his melon while listening to a general sketch and then made me go back, during the mushroom omelet, and take up every little detail that I could remember. It was useless to attempt any description of the two thugs because, as I told him, all that they had looked like had been a couple of noses. He seemed interested in the fact that the one guy had taken his mittens off and wanted to know just when, and how long afterward it had taken him to pull the gun out from under the reefer.

During his second cup of coffee he spread out the lecture on elementary physics, stressing especially some theory about two solids never yet having been able to occupy the same space, and then said:

"Bert, we will keep this to ourselves for a while."

"How can we? Look at me."

"You stumbled in the dark."

"You should have heard the steward on that one."

"The explanation will be accepted. It doesn't matter what they think as long as they do not know the truth before this evening. I refer principally to District Attorney Seward and the police."

While I finished my own mushroom omelet, he gave me the schedule for the day. He said, which was news to me, that the medical examiner had released Jettwick's body and that Miss Jettwick had decided to have the funeral that afternoon. Emberry, he said, had given him the information last night after dinner. Miss Jettwick wanted the funeral to be as swift and as private as possible because of the circumstances of her brother's death, which was reasonable when you consider the mob of morbid curiosity seekers that the funeral of any murdered person draws.

A brief ceremony was to be held at the Jepson Funeral Chapel and the interment would follow immediately at Woodlawn. This would occupy the hours between two and five o'clock in the afternoon.

Moon had informed Emberry that neither he nor I would attend. He felt reasonably certain that during that period *Trade Wind* would be empty both of suspects and the police.

"I shall want," he said, "a diver."

Sometimes I can do nothing but repeat, so I repeated, and said:

"A diver?"

"Yes, Bert. Please have one here with his equipment by half past two. Charter a boat for him to work from, and whatever else he may require. He is to be prepared to search the bottom of the river beneath the hull of this yacht."

"What's he to look for?"

"We will tell him that just before he descends. Naturally what those two men were grappling for last night was the missing black steel box. I want it. I want to open it and examine its contents before either Seward or the police get hold of it. Arrange some satisfactory and speedy getaway for us to use as soon as the box is brought up."

That wasn't all. Oh, no. I was to put the goad on Jimmy Singer and tell him that the dope on Senator Blackman's wife and on Jeffry Smith had to come through by express. Then Jimmy was to have a man aboard *Trade Wind* at a quarter past two with some powdered graphite and a camera. Finally, I was to make an appointment for some hour before lunch with the pastor of the church over in Chelsea which Myron Jettwick had started going to after he got religion. In the meanwhile Moon planned to catch up on his reading of *A High Wind in Jamaica*.

Well, I left *Trade Wind* and boarded *Coquilla* to do telephoning in private from there, also to evade comments on the model of Mount Everest which I was carrying on my head. *Coquilla's* crew have been trained to indifference to things like that.

The diver was simple. The Classified Telephone Directory listed three concerns, and the Manhattan Underseas Contracting Company listened to my story and accepted the job with the nonchalance of a bakery taking an order for cake. The only difference was in the bill.

I checked with Jimmy Singer. Nothing had been turned up immediately on Jeffry Smith, but Senator Blackman's wife had been easily located. Her home was in Akron, Ohio, but she had been spending the holiday season in New York and was at present registered at the Waldorf. Naturally, nothing as yet had come through on her dossier during the past fifteen years beyond the easily ascertained facts that she and Senator Blackman had been divorced thirteen years ago, that neither had remarried, and that she was a hot shot locally in Akron in society, all the clubs, movements, charities and drives. She had no children, but had evolved a book of verse entitled *Women Pirates of Today*. Just a bee.

Arranging the getaway for the black steel box and Moon and me, providing the diver brought it up, was more complicated, as most getaways are. In spite of Moon's feeling that Seward's office and the police and the press would be covering the funeral and ignoring the yacht, there seemed no sense in taking that chance.

As somebody always says, two bowstrings are better than one, so why not cover the river as well as the land? I called up Moon's chauffeur, Muddy—his face has the color of a delta—and told him to hold the Daimler ready for a quick start from two-thirty on, and to park himself on the avenue, one block south of Wharf House.

Then I went up to Captain Walsh's quarters—he's the master of *Coquilla*—and asked him to have the speedboat lowered and manned and held ready alongside the portside landing ladder by half past two. I asked him to put in the speedboat a length of thin strong line with a small grapple fastened at one end.

Both Seward and the police have an annoying habit of blowing their tops when any evidence connected with a case is even temporarily snatched away from under their noses. They have even been known to take steps. So the idea was this: if we did have any official spectators, and the diver located the box, he wasn't to bring it to the surface but was to make it fast to the loose end of the thin, strong line. Then he was to bring the small grapple end to the surface and inconspicuously, if a diver can be inconspicuous, place the grapple in the speedboat. Then he was to submerge again, as if he were still looking for whatever object he was supposed to want.

Of course, while any official observer would still be watching and waiting for the diver to come up again with treasure-trove, Moon and the grapple and I would be gently away in the speedboat, dragging the steel box behind us, and getting it aboard as soon as we were out of sight, and then hitting as fast as the screw would turn for the north shore of Long Island. I fixed it with Jimmy Singer to have a fast car waiting at a landing near Oyster Bay, and that was that. It all seemed to me to drip with honey.

As for the pastor of the church in Chelsea, that was reasonably simple, too. A sad-voiced woman housekeeper told me, after a hold-the-line-please of five minutes, that the Reverend Munster Grant would receive Mr. Moon and Mr. Stanley in the parsonage at eleven o'clock.

I shook Moon loose from *A High Wind in Jamaica* in time and we taxied over to a high-stooped house in the Twenties, west of Tenth Avenue. It was a fine old building, having a back yard that abutted the rear of the church on the block north of it. Moon had asked me on the ride over whether everything was satisfactorily arranged for the afternoon and I said that it was, and that was all. He dislikes bothering about the mechanics of any plan, unless they don't work, and part of my job is to see that they do.

A middle-aged maidservant ushered us into a high-ceilinged parlor, darkened by heavy curtains and drapes at the windows, and shadowed like any Karloff set with a couple of candelabras that were lighted and standing on an Empire table. Moon said that the several portraits and paintings on the long dark walls were early Flemish, which was all right with me, as you couldn't see them anyhow.

A plump old man with soft white hands and a Roman collar came in shortly and introduced himself as the Reverend Munster Grant. He asked us to sit down, and picked out for himself a Spanish throne chair covered in faded maroon velvet and showing a worn embroidered crest.

"Gentlemen?"

"You can help us, Mr. Grant," Moon said. "I understand that Mr. Myron Jettwick attended your church during the last month of his life. If you will overlook the impertinence of my prying into a man's spiritual affairs, I would appreciate a frank opinion from you on Mr. Jettwick's sincerity. I assure you the question is one of importance."

"Of importance to whom, sir?"

"To a determination of the guilt of his murderer."

The Reverend Grant drew a finely carved snuffbox from a pocket of his jacket, picked out a pinch, and sniffed deeply. Then he lightly waved a cambric handkerchief across his lapels. It was something that I had always wanted to see done, in the flesh.

"There are two kinds of sincerity," the Reverend Grant said. "There is the one which is rooted innately in a man from his birth, and the other which is inspired through the hysteria of some shocking moment. Mr. Jettwick's was of the latter. It was nonetheless genuine, for all that."

"Did you talk with him very much, Mr. Grant?"

"Yes. He invariably came here to my chambers after morning services and would stay sometimes an hour, sometimes two." You could hardly see the Reverend Grant's dark eyes in the heavy shadows. "Precisely what is it that you want to know, Mr. Moon?"

"The things that he told you about his past."

"I have not the right to disclose them. If generalities will be of assistance to you, Mr. Jettwick did have a genuine fear of some spiritual retribution. His conscience was bothering him. What he sought from the church, from me, was an insurance policy for his soul."

The Reverend Grant exposed placid palms.

"I gave him what comfort I could."

"Let me ask this. Did his conscience bother him in reference to his divorced wife or her son?"

"Among other things, yes. He felt a compulsion to make amends. He would reiterate that he had treated her more harshly than he had evidently come to consider just."

"In what way?"

"I cannot be franker than that."

"Were the amends because he had wronged her, or because he had punished her too severely for her having wronged him?"

Chimes started going from some place in the house. The Reverend Grant stood up. He seemed to be studying Moon for a moment patiently and with a sort of meekness.

"There is only one suggestion I can make that may possibly help you, Mr. Moon."

"Yes?"

"If your own resources, or the resources of the police will enable you to do so, I would locate a man by the name of Jeffry Smith."

The way he said it was like the end of a ghost story. You know the sort—where you get a cold chill from a "*Boo!*"

TWELVE

TWO-THIRTY—AND AFTER

I dropped Moon at *Trade Wind* and then went over to *Coquilla* to fix up some added frills that I'd remembered were necessary for the get-away. I asked Captain Walsh to have heavy ulsters, wool helmets, and fleece-lined gloves stowed in the speedboat for Moon and me, and to have Walter fix up a thermos jug of hot spiced rums to go, too.

Then I went to Harry Lochbittern's cabin and saw him. Harry is *Coquilla*'s chief engineer, and Moon hired him on the waterfront of New Orleans after Harry had reformed from some happy and wonderful years ashore as a safe-cracker of nationwide repute.

I told Harry to pack a brief case with the odds and ends he'd need for opening a small steel box, to be done in his inimitable fashion so that nobody would know he had done it, and to wrap himself up warm and take a stand on the landing stage of Wharf House from two-thirty on. I would signal him from the deck of *Trade Wind*. If no official observers showed, one signal would mean for him to climb into the Daimler. If the law did show, another signal would mean for him to get into the speedboat and wait for us there.

The short stroll from *Coquilla* to *Trade Wind* was uneventful except for a word or two with Elizabeth, who was pacing mournfully up and down the starboard side of the main deck. She brightened a lot on seeing my head and said, "So you hit a door in the dark?" and I said, "However did you guess, Miss Schuyler?" and she said she hoped it would do Bruce some good, and I said I was tired of having my very painful duck egg considered as a jumping-off-place for other people's good luck, and went below.

I did not, due to the duck egg, join the rest for luncheon but had some curried pigeons with rice, plus Pilsner, sent in to the living room, and read the morning and early-afternoon editions while eating and drinking same.

They all sang the same song under similar scare-heads: Bruce was this and Bruce was that, and his mother's scandalous past was carefully dusted and shot off again, and advanced as the alleged motive for Bruce's alleged cooling of his uncle, and not a sheet but had him already half-fried in the electric chair come spring.

Elizabeth and her mother came in for a pretty basketful of public-ity, too. Elizabeth's coming-out riot at the Waldorf was revived, vintage bottle by vintage bottle, and the fact of her having suddenly canceled the main joint of her first social season for a lengthy cruise to the ordinary Caribbean on an ordinary yacht was put down in cold type for anybody to dope out as he liked.

The bright, redheaded, little witless had furthermore given what could pass, legally, as an interview to Lettice Laceheart, whose column in the *Daily Review* was the saccharin in the female portion of the town's morning coffee.

Elizabeth told me about it after I'd told her what I thought about it. All she'd done, Elizabeth said, had been to yell a few words from *Trade Wind*'s deck down to a nice-looking young woman covered with skinned leopards, who had yelled a few casual questions up to her from the land-ing stage, and had then asked a dyspeptic prize fighter in a turtle-neck sweater to take Elizabeth's picture.

What she had as a result to paste in her scrapbook was, in part, this:

> "The dashing young debutante, wearing vivid green and mink, refused to admit that she had known Bruce Jettwick previously to their meeting on New Year's Eve aboard his uncle's palatial yacht, the *Trade Wind*. In spite of this denial, Miss Schuyler did admit to such a deep interest in the handsome young murder suspect, and radio singer, that it made your correspondent wonder whether they mightn't have known each other rather well in, shall we say, some other incarnation"

(Elizabeth's version of this: LETTICE LACEHEART, *shouting*: "How long have you known Bruce Jettwick?"
ELIZABETH, *shouting*: "Only met him last night."
LETTICE, *shouting*: "Like him?"
ELIZABETH, *shouting*: "Certainly I like him. Who wouldn't?")

> "When asked whether she believed in his innocence, Miss Schuy-ler pressed back tears from her deep violet-blue eyes, and said: 'Yes.' She blushed and seemed confused when I then asked her whether she would wait for Bruce Jettwick, no matter how many years it might be, and providing he escaped the dread, full penalty of the law. My heart ached to see the tears spring back again, to see her cheeks flush a deeper red, and to hear the words choke in her mink-wrapped throat as, speechless, she gave me one poignant parting glance and fled with her breaking heart down to the seclusion of her luxurious cabin."

All of which was nice fast going and not a libel in it.

Moon came down from lunch at half past one and told me I hadn't missed anything as it had been like most pre-funeral luncheons, fairly dead pan and not much general appetite, and with Mrs. Schuyler tossing the conversational pigskin for some lateral passes of a here-today-and-gone-tomorrow nature. Moon asked me to give the bunch time to get on their things and start for the Jepson Funeral Chapel, and then to go up on deck. He said he would cut one quarter-hour from his after-lunch nap in order to give instructions to Jimmy Singer's man who was due on board at a quarter past two with the powdered graphite and the camera. Moon told me to stay on deck, but to send the man down and to tell the man to wake him up; then he went into the bedroom and closed the door.

I got into a British warm which I'd picked up five years ago when we were in London, and which refused to wear out, and went on deck. Snow was with us again, sifting down from a lead-nickel sky and stinging along on a fresh wind from the northeast.

My watch said a quarter of two. Evidently the next half-hour called for giving the impression of a fresh-air fiend being robustly exhilarated by a whole lot of deck-pacing and fresh air.

You could walk right around the deck housing on *Trade Wind*'s main deck, so I did just that, eying the landing stage of Wharf House while steaming along the starboard side, and eying the river for the Manhattan Underseas Contracting Company's tug while dittoing the portside.

I thought, for a while, that the landing stage was innocent of dicks or cops, but on the fifth lap around I spotted a stern-eyed young thing in the plainest of clothes gloomily chewing gum just inside the plate-glass door leading into Wharf House's river entrance. He had his hat on, and you knew he was holding himself on leash for any tail job that came along. There were probably three or four more just like him inside in the superintendent's office, and playing the fingers' game, while he chewed his gum and kept a lookout on the yacht.

That meant the speedboat and the river, and very soon indeed things began to happen. Jimmy's man showed up right on the dot at a quarter past two. I sent him down to Moon and then forgot about him, while wishing for four sets of eyes because Captain Walsh was getting ready to lower the speedboat over on *Coquilla*, the diver company's tug was steaming up and would soon drop her hook alongside, Harry Lochbittern was sedately walking down *Coquilla's* gangplank, well wrapped up and with the brief case in his hand, and Young Chewing Gum had opened the plate-glass door and was now outside on the landing stage and getting interested. Cops, and don't I know it, develop a sixth sense which tells them when something tinted is in the wind.

I signaled Harry first, by leaning on the starboard rail, lighting a cigarette, taking a couple of drags and then dropping the cigarette into the river. He went handsomely Theatre Guild, fumbled around in his overcoat pocket as though he'd forgotten something, shrugged, went back to the gangplank and boarded *Coquilla* again. I knew he would shortly go down the portside landing ladder and get into the speedboat, so he was off my mind.

A representative of the Manhattan Underseas Contracting Company boarded *Trade Wind* from the landing stage. He introduced himself as Oscar Wickstrom, one of the partners. He had the placid type of Swedish face which is such a fine mask for a solid boxful of intelligent shrewdness. He was getting a good stiff price for the job and knew it, so he listened carefully to the setup and raised no objections to the play about the thin line, grapple and speedboat, but told me to leave everything to him. He returned to the landing stage, boarded a small boat from the tug and went out in her to the tug.

Moon hit the deck around then, and Jimmy's man was with him. They shook hands at the gangplank, and Jimmy's man went ashore and I didn't see him again for another three-quarters of an hour when I happened to notice him bobbing around in a rowboat, a phenomenon which there was no time to figure out at the moment. Anyhow, by that time, if you forgot the snow and biting wind, the river in the neighborhood of Wharf House looked like Henley.

Moon looked smug when I told him everything was smooth and said, "That's nice, Bert," in the way he does when he's got some egg trick of his own up his sleeve.

The lad from Center Street had the wind well up by now and had come aboard. He joined us.

"Nasty day, Mr. Moon," he said.

"Yes, isn't it."

"I'm Duffy, from Homicide."

"How-do-you-do, Mr. Duffy. Have you met my secretary, Bert Stanley?"

"No."

"Mr. Duffy, Mr. Stanley."

Mr. Duffy and Mr. Stanley shook gloves. Mr. Duffy then squinted some snow out of his eyes.

"May turn out to be a blizzard, Mr. Moon."

"It might."

"If it did, we'd form a society."

"I beg your pardon?"

"You know, just like that bunch did that went through the blizzard back in 'eighty-eight."

"Ah?"

"And we'd have a dinner once a year. I like dinners. You ought to taste the job that Mrs. Duffy can do on a goose."

"My compliments to Mrs. Duffy."

"Thanks."

You could all but spot the chapter on "Psychological Approach" in the manual which this line of lather must have come from, First-lull-your-quarry-with-small-talk-before-pouncing; that sort of thing.

Well, Moon being presumably fully lulled, Young Hopeful got down to tacks. He nodded over at the tug and said, "That looks like a diving outfit."

"Yes, doesn't it?"

"Having some diving done, Mr. Moon?"

"I thought I might."

"Here?"

"Here."

"What for?"

"Now there, Mr. Duffy, you've got me. I don't know."

"Huh."

"I mean I don't know in the sense that the man will dive simply on a general hunt for clues."

"Such as?"

Moon did a fine job of looking slightly annoyed and embarrassed. It got my full vote for the Academy award.

"Mr. Duffy, I have no reason for not being perfectly frank," he said, and God help Mr. Duffy. "We are sparing no expense and leaving no stone unturned in our efforts to establish my client's innocence."

"Still what?"

"One of the pieces of evidence that I am positive will clear Bruce Jettwick is the murder gun. The ownership of that gun will be traced, and the true criminal apprehended. So far the police have not been able to locate that gun. I have employed a diver to search the river bed in the vicinity of the scene of the crime. Mr. Duffy, you may draw your own conclusions."

If Duffy had had a lighted rocket in his hip pocket he couldn't have left *Trade Wind* quicker.

"A fine thing!" I said, and meant it. "He'll have the harbor police up here in ten minutes."

"I want them."

"Are you crazy?"

"Yes. I saw that man right after lunch, before I went below. I knew it was inevitable that we would have to consider the police."

"But I've a plan for that."

"I'm certain it will dovetail with mine. Remember, Bert, that nothing makes a dog less attentive to surrounding activities than throwing him a good meaty bone to chew on."

"That is just dandy. Where's the bone?"

He smiled in that polite way that makes me want to strangle him, and asked me to instruct him in the steps he would have to take for our getaway. I told him, and he said "Excellent, excellent," and walked down the gangplank and over toward *Coquilla* with me in tow. We went aboard, and Moon asked me to wait for him in the speedboat while he went below and picked up a few things he wanted in his quarters.

It was ten minutes of three.

Coquilla's speedboat is a honey. She's stout enough to stand a moderately heavy sea without pounding to pieces, and her twin Bhudas will shoot her up to sixty and hold her there against most weather. The two men who always handle her were in the forward cockpit with Harry Lochbittern and his brief case between them. I got into the after cockpit, with its own windshield and spray hood, and checked on the line, grapple, ulsters, thermos jug and so forth.

Moon came down and got in, and we shoved off and idled over to the tug. Oscar Wickstrom was leaning over its rail. The snow was getting thicker, and I asked him how the diver would be able to see anything on that sort of a day, and he said something about a modern underwater light and told me not to worry. I handed up the thin line and grapple, while we innocently so chatted, and he said that the diver was all set to go down. He advised us to make fast to the tug so that the diver would know just where to locate us when he came to pull his trick.

Moon said to Wickstrom, "I suggest that the diver bring up two or three objects from the bottom of the river and give them to us before he brings up the grapple; say, anything at all that he may find."

"A good idea, Mr. Moon. I'll tell him."

We made fast and were nicely set by the time that the returns showed up from harbor "A," thanks to Mr. Duffy. They were a couple of harbor police launches, and District Attorney Seward and Assistant Police Commissioner McGilvray were aboard one of them, and a World Movietone Newsreel cameraman with his apparatus was with the lads in the other.

Moon spotted the newsreel man and said:

"It couldn't be working out better, Bert."

There are moments when utter disgust makes me speechless, and I thought of Moon's remark that the hours between two and five would find the vicinity of *Trade Wind* free of suspects and of official observation, and was speechless.

The diver was lowering himself by a ladder over the side of the tug. He looked like nothing I thought a diver ought to look like, having been accustomed through pictures to objects resembling vertical tanks that are swung overboard by cranes. This guy looked almost naked in comparison as he wore nothing but a rubber suit, heavy boots, a modern helmet and some gadgets strapped to his back. Wickstrom later told me that the depth and pressure were nothing to speak of right there, and that that was all the equipment the man needed. There was no air tube, and nothing but a safety line to yank him up by.

The harbor police boat with Seward and McGilvray maneuvered into the best position for getting in on the newsreel shot of the diver making his first submerge. Then it slid alongside us and McGilvray said:

"What was the idea of not tipping us off about this, Moon?"

"I couldn't see the sense in bothering you, McGilvray. At the best it's nothing but a wild-goose chase."

"It's a pretty expensive one, I'd say."

"My client has enough money to avoid any sparing of expense."

"Don't I know it." McGilvray added grimly, "I warn you, Moon, we're on hand to take over anything your diver brings up."

"McGilvray, for your own sake, do not be absurd. That man is a licensed diver in my private employ engaged on a private job. If in his search he should produce any object which either you or Mr. Seward can prove to me is evidentially connected with the murder of Myron Jettwick, you have the right to demand it and I shall turn it over to you cheerfully. Whatever else he may find is his business and mine."

"That man—what's-his-name—"

"Mr. Duffy."

"Duffy; he said you were diving for the murder gun."

"Quite right. For the murder gun, and for whatever else the diver may find."

There was just enough smoke in this screen to confuse McGilvray and he started to look fierce, but then suddenly broke into a corncob smile, which puzzled me until I saw that the diver was coming up, and that the newsreel cameraman was cranking, and that McGilvray was moving stage center as closely as the police launch would let him.

It was a battered child's go-cart.

The diver clung to the speedboat and reached the go-cart up to Moon, who lifted it solemnly into the cockpit and set it down. The diver submerged again. Moon gestured toward the go-cart and looked inquiringly over at McGilvray, only to meet a chill and formal silence.

Object number two was a rusted frying pan with some holes in it.

Moon smiled. Seward smiled. McGilvray had to smile because the camera was cranking again. Harry Lochbittern started to laugh himself sick. He has no sense of restraint whatsoever.

This time the diver stayed down much longer than he had before. Ten minutes passed, while the snow got thicker and the wind from the northeast had ice in its teeth. The launch with the cameraman aboard moved closer to the other police boat, and the cameraman shouted that he'd practically have to take close-ups to get anything at all. You could see that this didn't irritate McGilvray one bit.

Five more minutes passed.

The way Moon worked it was real art. He had been sitting quietly on the stern seat, with his left hand hanging over the speedboat's side. He didn't move, even when the diver's helmet broke water. He didn't move until the diver had tossed the small grappling hook over the speedboat's stern and into the cockpit. The diver submerged again immediately. Then Moon stood up, then crouched swiftly beside the grappling hook.

McGilvray almost fell overboard in his hurry to see what was up.

"What's that?" McGilvray shouted.

Moon held it up.

"A grappling hook."

"The hell with that. I mean the thing you picked off it—by God, it's a gun! Hand that gun over and be damned quick about it, Moon."

Again Moon did a fine job which blended anger, frustration, and regret. The police launch swept alongside, and Moon handed the dripping revolver over to McGilvray.

"Would you like the grappling hook too, McGilvray?"

"No, smarty. You can keep it for a souvenir."

"Thanks," said Moon.

The fade-out was a sweetheart. Harry Lochbittern quietly loosed our line from the tug, the twin Bhudas started purring, and gently as a snowflake we opened water between us and the two police boats. I like to remember my last glimpse of them, just before we gently pulled the black steel box on board and stowed it safely in the cockpit under an ulster. The newsreel cameraman was cranking away and shouting to McGilvray:

"No, Commissioner, don't point it at the lens—No, no, not straight—sideways so the audience can see it's a gun—it's the murder gun World Movietone wants, Commissioner—sideways—*flat*, Commissioner—okay—okay—okay—"

They never knew we were gone until the snowfall had blurred us, and by then we were hitting a full sixty and nothing in that man's harbor could have caught us. Moon didn't need to tell me about the gun. It was an old crock with its numbers filed off that had been given him by an admirer, a second-story man in Melbourne. I'd seen Moon when he had slipped it out of his overcoat pocket and had held it over the speedboat's side, so that when he untangled it from the grapple it would be nice and wet.

I uncorked the thermos jug and passed it around. Walter had done a good job. It was hot, rightly spiced, and very fine rum.

THIRTEEN

REWARD: $10,000

Harry Lochbittern, with a fine show of acrobatics, joined us with his briefcase in the after cockpit. Sheltered by the spray hood from the terrific drive of wind, spume and snow, he sat on the floor boards and took a look at the black steel box's lock with a tenderness that only a mother could display toward a long-mislaid child. Moon asked him whether he could accomplish anything while the speedboat was doing its rumba through the seas, and Harry looked hurt and said forget it, and picked out some small fine instruments and got to work.

Twenty minutes later, Moon joined Harry on the floor boards and got ready to examine the papers in the opened box. It was a good box, self-sealing against fire and water, and none of the papers had been hurt. Moon complimented Harry both on his artistry and expedition and sent him, blushing, back to the stern seat and me, and the jug of hot spiced rums.

You had to admire the care with which Moon worked. He put on a pair of thin leather gloves, and read through the contents of the box. He put in his inner coat pocket an envelope containing a single sheet of note paper covered with script, three typewritten letters with their envelopes and something that looked like a contract.

He returned the other papers to the box and motioned Harry to join him. He told Harry to lock the box and to wipe it clean of fingerprints. He told him to return with it in the speedboat and, under cover of the complete darkness which would have fallen by then, to drop the box overboard alongside of *Trade Wind* before bringing the speedboat up to *Coquilla* and having her swung aboard.

Moon came back and sat down. He took off the thin gloves and threw them into the Sound, again taking no chances, in that their pattern or some slight defect in their surface might be developed from the papers and traced.

My face was all set with a bright and receptive look which was completely wasted because Moon lapsed into his impersonation of a clam and stayed that way until we left the speedboat and picked up the car outside of Oyster Ray. Moon pried his lips enough apart to tell the driver to hustle us to the Manning, and then cemented them together again.

The Manning is a small residential hotel in midtown Manhattan which Moon has so far succeeded in using as a quiet retreat when he doesn't want to be bothered either officially or socially. It still retains brass railings for its red-carpeted staircases, two openwork elevators with a shuddering speed of one vertical mile per hour, a staff of young lads of sixty, and a very good office safe.

It was half past five when we got there. Moon dismissed the car and we went inside. He asked Mr. Murgatroyd, the desk clerk, for a manila envelope. He put the papers he had taken from the steel box in it, sealed it, wrote his name on it, and told Mr. Murgatroyd to hold it for him in the office safe and not to deliver it to anyone but Moon himself or me.

After that and some seasonal greetings of a social and financial nature were attended to we went out into the darkness and the snow, netted a taxi, drove to Wharf House and boarded *Trade Wind*. The bunch were all back from the funeral, and we joined them in the main saloon where very good Mauser cocktails, sherry, and caviar were going the rounds.

Once again my esteem for Miss Jettwick hit a new high, because if anything can rub out the pall of a funeral a Mauser cocktail will. I hadn't had one for years. You make them with a half jigger of Italian vermouth, a half jigger of dry gin, one barspoonful of apple brandy. Shake.

Even without the Mausers they were all agog, as word had been given them of the diving operations during their absence, and the retrieving from the river bottom of what was still being accepted as the murder gun. Thanks to Elizabeth the duck egg on my head had also been bruited around and came in for its moment of attention, too.

I hated to see that look of hope on Helen Jettwick's face. They call it radiant, and you knew she was figuring that as soon as the murder gun was checked down at headquarters both McGilvray and Seward would see that they had make a mistake, and Bruce would be released from the Tombs and come home to her.

Moon told her privately as soon as he could that it wasn't as simple as that, but he told her to be of good heart. The phrase must have struck her one hundred percent because she studied Moon's eyes for a moment, and the radiance started to come back again on a firmer basis, if you know what I mean.

As for the rest of them, if one of them did happen to be the lad or lass we were after, he or she was doing a fine cover job of ignoring the fact that Moon's diver might, while scuttling about on the river bottom, have come across the black steel box.

Even my pet suspect, Spider McRoss, stuck strictly to the finding of the gun and was very eager to know just how it would affect Bruce's chances for a quick exit from the cage. Wallace Emberry answered that one. He was staying on for dinner, after having come back with them from the funeral, and he told McRoss that unless the gun could be traced to its last owner It wouldn't do any more good than his own efforts had to obtain a writ of *habeas corpus* or to have Bruce turned loose on bail.

From the way his eyes popped you could tell that he was still good and mad because said efforts had resulted in nil.

I put the telescopic gaze on Mrs. Schuyler and could see nothing there, even though she did seem paler and less well preserved than usual, and what the Frogs call *distrait*. In fact, later, after the case was closed, when I thought back on all the good eye work I wasted during that cocktail hour, I was one point this side of ditching my career of chasing nuts and criminals with Moon and taking up simple bartending again, because Moon knew right at that minute exactly why Myron Jettwick had been murdered, and was morally certain as to who had fired the gun.

A steward announced District Attorney Seward just then, which shortly focused my duck egg into the spotlight. Seward came in with his overcoat on, his hat in his hand, and several late editions tucked under his arm. His smile and greetings had the temperature of an icebox cake all ready to serve. He spread the newspapers out on a table and though everybody collected to look at them the verbal play turned into a duet between him and Moon, like any of the duets in *La Tosca* that have the true lethal touch.

Well, there were some good pictures of the diving act, with McGilvray's puss grinning front and center in each, but what Seward was hot about was a brief stop press about my shy breakfast in the living room with bump. The reporter had squeezed the bald facts from the room steward and had suggested the rest, hitting a bull's-eye in an alleged supposition that I had been attacked during the night, and pinning it on the blood I'd left on the face towels when I'd washed it off my head before going in to see Moon.

"I want the facts about that," Seward said, opening the duet.

Moon answered for me.

"It is true. Mr. Stanley was attacked. He was struck on the head by the butt of a revolver held in the hand of an unidentified man."

"Why wasn't I informed of it?"

"The injury was inconsequential, Mr. Seward."

I restrained myself perfectly. So did Seward.

"You know I don't mean that. The attack on Mr. Stanley certainly must have had its bearing on the murder of Myron Jettwick. Tell me what happened, please." Moon did.

"I take it," Seward said when Moon was finished, "your presumption that the men were grappling for something was the reason for your sending down a diver?"

"Yes, Mr. Seward."

"For a gun?"

"For the murder gun."

"For that relic you palmed off on McGilvray?"

"Relic?"

"That's right, Mr. Moon, relic. Our ballistics man reported that it hadn't been fired in years. It didn't even have a firing pin."

"I don't see the reason for this touch of heat, Mr. Seward. Surely you aren't holding me responsible for the futility of the diver's search? That gun was turned over to Commissioner McGilvray the instant he demanded it. If I remember correctly, it was still dripping."

"Dripping, yes, but no mud."

"Mud?"

"Yes, mud. River-bottom mud."

Moon went ancestral and became Southern patience itself.

"Surely any silt or bottom mud would have been washed from the gun while the diver was bringing it to the surface."

"The ballistics man doesn't believe so. He said some would have seeped in and stuck there. Furthermore, we've questioned the diver, and he refuses to make a positive statement that he did bring the gun up to the surface. He admits that he carried up the grapple, but doesn't know whether the gun was caught on it or not."

"Odd how things like that happen."

"Very odd."

"Especially odd when you realize that those two men last night in the rowboat must have hooked the gun with the grapple at the exact moment when Mr. Stanley shouted at them and they dropped the line overboard in their fright."

Seward got a good wine red under the handsome sun tan he'd brought back with him from Bermuda.

"I suppose that is the way the story will have to stand, Mr. Moon."

"I don't see how it could be otherwise."

"We're sending our own diver down, of course."

"Of course. I left as soon as Commissioner McGilvray impounded the gun. I saw nothing further to wait for. Did my man bring up anything else?"

The wine became burgundy.

"Just a dress form."

"Oh, surely not! Of the hourglass type?"

"Of the hourglass type." Seward turned several pages of the *Daily Review* and pointed to a full-page ad. "If you considered Mr. Stanley's injuries so inconsequential, in the sense that you felt them of no interest to my office or the police, what is the meaning of that?" The "that" was the full-page ad, which consisted of a ten-thousand-dollar reward for information leading to the identity or arrest of one or both of the two men who had attacked me from the rowboat. The information was to be sent or given directly to Moon and would be treated as strictly confidential. Moon listed his address as *Trade Wind*, located the yacht as being moored at Wharf House, and included the number of the land telephone installed on board.

The reward was all news to me, and I couldn't dope out why Moon had done it. The reason he gave to Seward was, of course, just so much meringue. He said: "I have every respect for the ability of the police department and for your own, Mr. Seward. I have a greater respect for the efficacy of money. Plenty of money, under which classification I would place ten thousand dollars. It is the type of sum that not only gets action, but gets it quick."

And the funny part of it is that Moon, in his devious way, was right.

FOURTEEN

A WOMAN POSSESSED

Seward left with a parting crack that he hoped Moon had enjoyed his sail down the harbor, or wherever he'd gone in the blizzard, and complimented him on having introduced a new winter sport, although doubting whether it would receive much favor among the yachting fraternity. Moon said he accepted the compliment in the spirit in which it was meant, and we went below to dress for dinner.

I sat on the edge of the bathtub and tried, as one says, to pierce his reticence by conjecturing on the reward stunt while he shaved and made the usual faces and grunts which go with lather and a razor. Moon uses the straight kind. He claims that they're here to stay.

I said what did he think we were up against, a gang? So far we had the two bundled dopes in the rowboat, Bruce in jail, Madame President Schuyler with her duds and a hat on before the murder dawn, the wife of Senator Blackman far from her Akron home during the festive season and holed in at the Waldorf, Rat Jeffry Smith any place, and my own nominee, Spider McRoss.

Providing the two boatmen with the grapple weren't principals, who had hired them? Surely the bulk of our suspects were far too chic to be able to step out and pick up for a sum such an accomplished brace of maritime thugs for their dirty work? Moon asked me to shut up because, even though he'd mentally lowered the asbestos between us, just the sound of my voice had made him nick his chin.

He told me to go see the chief steward and arrange that whatever man was detailed to the small switchboard installed for land service be warned that any telephone call coming through for him, Moon, be plugged through immediately to the extension in our quarters, or to whatever other spot on the yacht Moon might happen to be. No questions were to be asked the caller, who was to be assured that Moon was on board and would be connected at once. The same general routine was to hold with anyone who came personally, and the man on deck watch was to be instructed of the fact.

After I had cleared that up, he wanted me to run over to *Coquilla* and gather ten thousand dollars in twenty five-hundred-dollar bills from the safe. He always keeps some cash on hand as he hates to be caught short, and insists that ready money is as important a weapon in his business as is a gun.

I began to get the feeling that it looked like a big night and thought enviously of hockey and football players with their head guards, shin guards, and scatter of Ostermoor padding, while running my errands and then coming back to Moon. I asked him where he wanted me to put the ten thousand dollars, and he told me to get into my dinner clothes and put the money in my pants pocket and to complete the ensemble by wearing my shoulder holster under the left armpit.

Dinner went along about as you would expect, with most topics of current interest being touched on, with the exception of Bruce. Emberry rehashed the funeral, and practically a blow-by-blow account of the pastor's eulogy of Myron Jettwick. Emberry alone of them seemed to have taken the old buzzard's death hard, and that looked strange, until you realized he'd not only been associated with Jettwick for years but had just lost, through Jettwick's death, what had probably been his fattest account. I did find out later, just as a whim of curiosity, that Jettwick's legal business had brought him in an average of ninety thousand bucks a year. In a case like that, I'd have felt pretty blue and grim myself.

Well, we'd struggled through some woodcock a la Talleyrand, with a green salad, and were spooning out a very good sabayon prepared, for a change, with Kirschwasser when a steward hustled in and handed Moon a folded note. It plugged Emberry in the middle of a Technicolor description of the funeral's floral arrangements. It plugged everybody with a good cold chill, even me.

Moon read the note quickly and then said to Miss Jettwick:

"This is from Mrs. Blackman, the former wife of Senator Blackman. She wants to see me. She asks me to apologize for the informality of coming on board, but says that her business is imperative."

It was the last name that any of us expected to hear. Helen Jettwick turned a sickly white. Miss Jettwick's nice friendly face hardened to a point where she looked like a different person. Emberry said, "What? What?" and popped his eyes. Elizabeth just looked blank. McRoss upset his glass of champagne on the table, and don't think I didn't put that little fact down in the book.

Mrs. Schuyler ran true to form and said, "Blackman? Wasn't she the woman on the *Leviathan*—oh my *dear!*" She reached some finger loads of square-cut rocks set in platinum across the table, and pressed

Helen Jettwick's cold hand in a gesture pleading for forgiveness. Oh yes indeed.

Moon turned to the steward and said:

"Where is Mrs. Blackman?"

"In the library, sir."

"Miss Jettwick, with your permission?"

"Certainly, Mr. Moon."

"Thank you. Come with me, please, Bert."

There are some people who look sunken in, and that's the way Mrs. Blackman looked. She seemed to have no raised places at all, just flat places with dents. Her clothes were more extreme and more expensive than a woman of similar position in New York would buy, and her hat probably set her back fifty bucks, which made it worth about ten thousand times its weight in gold. As of when there was gold. Her coat was chinchilla, and her perfume was that new kind that was bottled in a leather boot, only heaven knew why.

Moon introduced himself and me, and she looked us over fast in a cold, nervous way and said she wanted to confer with Moon in private. He gave her the usual rigmarole about me being completely confidential and very private and, having so reduced me to a par with one of the library's walls, asked her to speak up.

"Very well. Mr. Moon, the newspapers have informed me that Bruce Jettwick is your client. I am *liée* with your career as an investigator. I am satisfied that in all your cases you have believed in the innocence of your client, and that that has been a factor in your unbroken line of success. Unbroken to date."

The "to date" curdled the soft soap, of course, and Moon got very blue-grass-plantation and said, "I gathered from your note that you have some information for me, Mrs. Blackman?"

"It is my purpose to convince you that you will never expose the true murderer of Mr. Jettwick until you see her through my eyes."

"See who?"

"Helen Jettwick, naturally. Whether she herself or her son fired the gun is of little consequence. The driving power was hers. I firmly believe it was she. I also believe you will free Bruce and, by doing so, will free his mother, too. That is what I have come to prevent."

"Just why, Mrs. Blackman?"

"Would you feel charitable toward a woman who had ruined your life?"

"I am to infer that Mrs. Jettwick ruined yours? Is a life so easily ruined by the loss of a few jewels? And I understand they were recovered, and that you exacted full payment for their theft. I do not understand you, Mrs. Blackman."

"The jewels were nothing but a handle that I grasped to control her."

"To control her from what?"

My pencil was going like sixty while taking down this dialogue, for that's what it sounded like to me, sort of a hash made up of some problem plays and seasoned with a reminiscent dash of Clyde Fitch.

"I suppose, Mr. Moon, you have made yourself familiar through old newspaper files with that *Leviathan* scandal."

"Yes."

"They are incomplete. Let me fill in the gaps for you."

"Thank you. Tell me this, just how well did you get to know Mr. and Mrs. Jettwick on the way over?"

"My husband, the Senator, got to know her too well."

"In what way did the intimacy develop?"

"Via the cocktail lounge, mostly. They held a mutual interest in Clover Clubs that amounted to devotion. And my husband was then a very attractive man, Mr. Moon."

"Was Helen Jettwick the cause of your later divorce from him?"

"Indirectly, yes. He considered her a tragic and a maligned woman, even to a point where he flatly said that my attitude toward her was and had been cruelly indefensible. I think you will understand. I mean even after her trial and her divorce from Myron Jettwick she was always between us, almost physically so, if that doesn't put it too strongly. Finally, it seemed better that the Senator and I divorce each other on the usual blanketing grounds of incompatibility. That is why I say, Mr. Moon, that that woman ruined my life, and my home, and my entire happiness."

Well, what with chinchilla and the rest of her streamlined scenery, she certainly got no tears from me in her character of a cast-off glove, but her flat, bluish eyes had suddenly come alive in her flat face, and the thing they were blazing with was the finest eruption of downright hate I'd seen in years. Moon gave it a moment's inspection, too, and then said:

"Tell me your version of the thefts that took place during the voyage, Mrs. Blackman. The papers stated you were not the only victim."

"No, there were several, all in first class. Fanny Windemere lost an emerald dinner ring. Alice Colton lost a star sapphire pendant. She was that corset man's wife, his third, I think, and I lost my diamond bracelet."

"When was it taken?"

"It was stolen from my jewel box on the fourth night out. The Senator gave a dinner party in our suite, and there were ten guests, including Mr. and Mrs. Jettwick and Bruce. My husband could never get over a political aptitude for children. Anyhow, Bruce was quite large for his age and looked nearer fifteen than ten. There was the young daughter of another guest there as well. I wore my pearls that night—the Djavinski string—and the diamond bracelet was in the jewel box in a dresser drawer in my bedroom. There was a bathroom just beyond my bedroom doorway, and most of the guests went to it at some time or other during the evening. That gave Helen Jettwick her opportunity for the theft, of course."

"Did the bathroom have any door opening directly into your bedroom?"

"Yes, a door into the corridor, and one into the bedroom. It was terribly simple, really."

"How late did the party last?"

"The two children stayed until after nine, and the rest were there until around midnight. I was tired and completely fed up with the way my husband carried on"

"With Helen Jettwick?"

"Yes. It was the reason why I put the pearls back in the case without noticing the rest of the jewels. I didn't miss the bracelet until the following night when I wanted to wear it at the captain's dinner."

"Did you suspect Helen Jettwick?"

"No, not of being that sort of a thief. I did know, though, that she wanted money."

"How did you know, Mrs. Blackman?"

"By plain eavesdropping. I've never had the slightest scruple about it. I'm sure that you, as a detective, will sympathize with my point of view."

"To a point, Mrs. Blackman."

"Well, there were palm trees in the *Leviathan*'s lounge. She and the Senator were behind one, and I managed to be on its other side. It was after dinner and Mrs. Jettwick was well caught up on her daily quota of Clover Clubs and brandy. She said to the Senator: 'I can't stand it much longer. I'd leave him if I had any money to take care of Bruce with. I'd do almost anything to establish Bruce in some sort of a career.' Significant, wouldn't you say?"

"Completely so, on its surface."

"No, deeply so, too, Mr. Moon. The Senator asked her why she didn't divorce Myron Jettwick and get some sort of settlement, and she said: 'He wraps his cruelties up in kindness. He'd win out in any proceedings I might bring, and then I'd be penniless again and so would my son.' That's why she stole. My bracelet was worth twenty thousand dollars, and I imagine the rest of her loot totaled fifteen or so more. A very golden sort of nest egg, it struck me."

"A scene was reported on the dock when the jewels were recovered. The accounts were indecisive. Can you amplify it for me?"

"Vividly, Mr. Moon. The customs men were searching the luggage more carefully than usual because of the thefts. They found my bracelet shoved in the toe of a slipper among Helen Jettwick's things. The other stolen jewels were similarly hidden. Everyone heard the commotion up at 'J,' and I went there and identified the bracelet and insisted that Mrs. Jettwick be placed under arrest. That was when Bruce attacked me."

"Yes, I read of that."

"He was standing beside his mother, who was perfectly hysterical and denying the whole thing. So stupid, don't you think? I mean with the evidence of her guilt right there for anyone to see. Bruce leaped at me as I was demanding her arrest. He was like a savage beast and screamed the most terrible things. It terrifies me when I think of the average nice child's vocabulary. Then he turned on Myron Jettwick and said, 'If you let them touch my mother, I'll kill you.' Mr. Moon, I have never seen murder so plainly written on a human face."

"Oh, come, Mrs. Blackman—a child of ten."

"You doubt me? You doubt that it could linger over fifteen years? That the seed would grow?"

"Hate dies of attrition, Mrs. Blackman. Most elemental emotions do: love, grief, any of them at all. They have to be nurtured, to have the food of propinquity, in order to live."

Boy, did that woman pounce!

"Nurtured? My dear Mr. Moon, what else do you picture Helen Jettwick as doing during those years but fanning the flame?"

"Conjecture, Mrs. Blackman."

"Certainly, but based on her character as I knew it."

"A brief knowledge summed up during an ocean crossing."

"Surely, my dear man, you must see. See what his invitation to her two weeks ago must have meant. Every newspaper in town shrieks it as an alleged motive for Bruce's having killed him. Myron Jettwick wasn't signing a cruise invitation when he sent it to her. He was signing his own death warrant."

"Yes, you are right."

That stopped her.

"You really agree?"

"Yes, but not in the sense you mean."

"There is no other sense, no other meaning." (I'd heard of a woman "possessed," and saw one then.) "She and her son had built their lives up from ruin, built them financially and socially in a satisfactory enough way, when that quixotic desire of Myron's to forgive her her sins before he died made her fear a trick."

She was right there, of course, because I remembered McRoss's quote: Tell him that I am afraid to refuse.

"Surely, *surely* you see the picture, Mr. Moon? He had been relentless in his punishment of her fifteen years ago, and justly so. Her mind would reason thus: Myron has waited during all the years of our obscurity and penury for this moment when Bruce and I are on top only that the fall may be the greater when he tears us down). You know the all but fanatic code of censorship which obtains in radio. You know that Bruce's career would be ruined if he were exposed as the son of a woman whose thievery and divorce were a public scandal and a *cause célèbre*. As his career *has* been ruined. You know Helen Jettwick mistrusted Myron's magnanimity, and believed he was using it as a cloak to 'forgive her publicly' only to drag out her vicious past."

"Yes, I can understand Mrs. Jettwick reasoning like that."

"And you know this, too, Mr. Moon. That woman saw ruin staring her in the face. She believed that whether she accepted the invitation or not Myron Jettwick would speak, would expose the 'Unknown Troubadour' as her son. She came aboard this yacht in the blind fury of her hatred and passion to avenge a fate she considered inevitable. She had to suffer, yes. Bruce had to suffer. But in payment for that suffering, Myron Jettwick would die. If she could manage it in such a manner that they would escape with their necks, so much the better. Give up this case, Mr. Moon! For your own sake, for the sake of justice. I've come here to ask you to give it up."

"I can understand that bringing you here, Mrs. Blackman. What brought you to New York?"

"What?"

"Why did you leave your home in Akron during the holiday season, when normally you would be engaged in an essential social routine, and put up at a hotel in New York?"

"Why, the letter, of course."

"Letter?"

"Yes, from Myron Jettwick."

"Ah."

When Moon says "ah" it means "ah." Which means that it means no good for the party he says it to.

Flatty went on:

"He wrote and asked that I join him in this forgiveness feast, that I join him on the Caribbean cruise, that I add my voice in telling Helen

Jettwick that all was forgiven and forgotten. Mr. Moon, do you think the man was mad?"

"Having met you, Mrs. Blackman, I might be inclined to believe that way. So you did come to New York?"

"Yes, but the rest was absurd."

"When did you get here?"

"Last week."

"What day?"

"The day before New Year's Eve."

"I gather you had no intention of going on the cruise. Why did you come?"

"To dissuade him, to stiffen what had once been his determination to make that woman pay until the end."

"You saw him?"

"Yes."

"Here?"

"No, he came to the hotel."

"When?"

"Around four o'clock, on New Year's Eve."

"Your efforts were futile?"

"Quite"

"Your efforts at the hotel, I mean. Not later ones."

She gave that quite a take.

"There were no later ones, Mr. Moon. He left the hotel and I did not see him again."

"Then why didn't you return to Akron at once, Mrs. Blackman?"

What she would have said would have been important, very, but she had no chance to say it because the three of us saw that Helen Jettwick was in the room. The door was ajar and there was no telling how long she had been standing outside in the passageway and listening. It must have been for some time, and she couldn't have missed much, because she walked over to Mrs. Blackman and said, "Thank you for having come."

There are chills and chills, just as there are ice cubes so cold that they stick to your fingers where other ice cubes slide off. Mrs. Jettwick's voice gave me the sticky kind.

You could see that it gave them to Flatty, too, because she stood up in a hurry and pulled the chinchilla tighter about her. She said:

"I must be going."

"Thank you, too," Helen Jettwick's freezing plant went on, "for having been in New York on the night that Myron was shot. Has the value of an alibi occurred to you, Mrs. Blackman? If it hasn't, I'd consider it well"

Mrs. Blackman's exit was devoid of any social touch. I turned to toss flowers at Helen Jettwick but couldn't. She had slumped to the floor, and was out.

FIFTEEN

A HAND WITH A GUN

There was no time right then for a fireside chat with Moon as to why this and why that, because we'd just gotten Helen Jettwick revived with a swallow of brandy and well enough to be oh-my-poor-deared over by the women when a steward ran up to Moon and said a man wanted to talk to him on the telephone, and that the man's voice sounded shaky and scared.

Moon motioned me, and we hurried to the small switchboard in the coatroom off the main saloon. He took the call there, and held the earpiece of the headset so that I could listen in, too.

"Cotton Moon speaking."

"Listen, Mr. Moon, there's a small bar on Fifty-fourth Street between Second Avenue and Third. It's the only one on the north side of the block. Got that?"

"Yes."

"Have you the ten thousand dollars reward money in cash?"

"I have."

"Come to the bar and bring it with you. Keep this from the D.A. and the police or the deal's off."

"Very well."

"Be there within half an hour and come alone."

"I do not work alone. My secretary is always with me."

"Oh, him. Okay."

The punk hung up before I could think of an answer.

"Quick, Bert. Our coats."

We went ashore and picked up a cruising taxi, which was a break, because the snow was still coming down every which way and nobody who could avoid it was afoot. Moon said to Mr. Mike Guadopopolus—I always check a cabby's name and number from his license—"There is a bar on the north side of Fifty-fourth Street between Second Avenue and Third. Take us there, please."

The cab started south, and felt its way through the blizzard for twenty minutes before stopping alongside the curb. The trip under normal weather conditions would have taken six. We piled out and I paid the driver, and Moon said not to keep him.

We found ourselves before a café with a disillusioned canopy over its entrance. You could see a small bar through an iron-grilled window, with one of my ex-buddies polishing a glass behind it. The door was of solid oak and had an observation glass let into its upper panel as a hangover from the dear, dead, speakeasy days.

There was a small sprinkle of cash customers inside, a few at the bar, and the rest scattered around small tables in an extension in the rear. The joint was a typical neighborhood melting pot where the lads from Sutton Place bring their dogs and their glamour to the lads from the tenements. The pooches were on leashes, mostly tied to the legs of chairs, with one drowned dachshund checked at the bar rail and looking nostalgic for Vienna.

Moon picked out a wall table just at the end of the bar, and sat with his back against the wall so that he could watch both the street door and another door in the room's rear partition. The bartender finished polishing the glass, racked it, then lifted a flap in the bar and strolled over.

"What'll it be, folks?"

Moon said brandy and water, and I said the same.

"We got some Napoleon."

Moon smiled grimly and said:

"Prove it."

He came over with a tray after a while and put a bottle on the table, two ounce-and-a-half glasses, and two glasses half-filled with water and some ice.

"It's a shame to mix that stuff. I've got sniffers." Moon wrapped himself in Spanish moss and said:

"I prefer it this way, thank you. I am an iconoclast at heart."

"Oh, well, iconoclasm's fun for a while, but it gets tiresome like everything else and you skip it."

"Wait—you're a member of the Book-of-the-Month Club."

"I am. That will be two bucks."

I paid while Moon sat back and looked as if life were no longer worth living, and old First Edition returned to the bar's farther end and to a dreamy contemplation of the far-spaced passers-by along the snow-drifted street.

Five minutes later the door opened and a man came in.

He was a tall man and his large, pale face had an over-massaged look. He wore a derby and a dark chesterfield coat. His age might have been anything, and he wasn't one of the glamour boys because he had no Scottie, although you can't always tell.

He looked the joint over and then settled on Moon and me. He walked down to our end of the bar, which brought him within two or three feet of our table. He ordered a stinger.

Moon raised one eyebrow at me, which meant did Chesterfield look like one of the two men in the rowboat, and I raised both eyebrows at Moon, which meant he could search me and I still wouldn't know.

The man set his foot on the brass rail, took a cigar from an inner pocket and lighted it. He waited patiently while the bartender mixed his drink.

"That'll be fifty cents."

The man put a dollar bill on the bar, then pocketed his change. He sipped the stinger until the bartender had returned to the street end of the bar and had presented his back, while contemplating the empty world outside.

"Have you the money with you, Mr. Moon?"

The man didn't look at Moon. His lips hardly moved, but his whisper carried clearly to us, and no farther. A ten-year-old graduate of any neighborhood movie house could have tagged him as an ex-con.

"I have."

"Your primary purpose is to clear your client of having murdered his uncle, is it not?"

"Yes."

"The information which I am about to sell you will indicate a line of investigation which I think will do so."

"You know the conditions of the reward. Are you one of the two men who were in that rowboat?"

"No."

"Are you the man who hired them?"

"No."

"Will your information lead us to them?"

"No."

Moon finished his brandy.

"Come, Bert."

"Wait," the man said, in his grapevine whisper.

"I feel there is no sound reason for doing so."

"I am wanted by the police, and my life is not safe. I had nothing to do with Jettwick's murder. It is for another reason that I have to leave the country at once. I read your reward and decided that ten thousand dollars would see me through. I know nothing about the men in the rowboat and care less."

"There is definitely no purpose in prolonging this."

"Yes, there is." The man sipped some more of the stinger. "My name is Jeffry Smith."

Moon stopped pulling on his gloves.

"I thought you'd stay," Smith said. "My information is worth a lot more than ten thousand but, as I've indicated, I am being pressed and I cannot play the hand as it should be. In what denominations have you got the ten thousand?"

"There are twenty five-hundred-dollar bills."

Smith glanced toward the bartender's distant and stolid back.

"Let me see them. Just a minute—someone is coming in."

The street door opened, but nobody came in. A hand showed holding a revolver from which five shots blazed. The door closed on their echoes.

Jeffry Smith hit the floor and twitched and died, while two of the G-boys fainted and the drowned dachshund sat up and you could figure him thinking that perhaps Manhattan wasn't such a dull dump after all.

SIXTEEN

THINGS BEGIN TO WORK

Moon crooked a finger at the bartender and got us two more brandies, heaven alone knew how, because the joint was a madhouse what with Sutton Place and the tenements and the pooches all giving vent in their several ways, and only Smith being calm and quiet and no longer worried about anything at all. Moon had stopped me from hustling out to chase the sniper, as he had noted through the grilled window that a car had beaten it right after the shots, and I was, Moon said, no Balto. I missed this until I remembered the husky who had helped carry the serum to Nome.

Even with the blizzard a mob had begun to collect on the street, and two scout cars screamed up and emptied four policemen into our midst, while the cop on the beat kept the sightseers outside in check.

Moon identified himself, and identified Jeffry Smith, and suggested that District Attorney Seward and Assistant Police Commissioner McGilvray had better be summoned as the job unquestionably hooked up with the Jettwick case.

The usual spade work was done while we waited. All the cash customers gave names and addresses and occupations, when any, and a couple of the names would have shaken the social register to its stockings, while another couple would have had the same effect on a police blotter. It was wonderful the way nobody had seen a thing. Even the bartender remembered nothing but the hand and the gun. The sound of the five shots going off practically in his eardrums had blasted him out of his wits.

Some precinct boys and the headquarters' coterie got there before Seward or McGilvray, and one of the homicide dicks recognized Jeffry Smith under two aliases: Jock Severance and Jesse Stone. He knew his record, and told Moon that Smith's play consisted in petty embezzlements from well-off, middle-class widows. He knew that Smith was currently wanted for a job involving a synthetically helpless woman from Newark who had enough money, gumption and political influence to turn on the heat to a point where Smith must have realized he had hooked a barracuda and that some spot like Venezuela might be a good idea for a siesta.

Seward looked his own fresh-as-a-daisy self when he got there, and so did McGilvray, only his self was of the sour-puss order, and was right then very, very sour. You could tell he expected more antique gats.

Moon frankly gave them the setup, starting with Smith's phone call and ending with the fusillade. He suggested to Seward that if Seward cared to leave the current situation in McGilvray's capable hands and to return with us to *Trade Wind*, he, Moon, would like to talk with him, Seward, in a manner that might prove advantageous to both.

Seward agreed, and after we'd posed for a few family groups for the newspaper camera boys, the three of us shoved off in Seward's car, made *Trade Wind* and went below. Moon told me not to take off my coat, but would I mind sending the steward in with some scotch and soda, and then have the Daimler sent around to Wharf House and wait in it until he came out and joined me.

Moon always does that, chases me off when he wants to make a deal with any politician or official, they being temperamental that way about coming to any understandings when a third party is present who could later act as a witness. Moon's deals are never criminal, but some of them do verge on stretching the fine inner tubing of the law, and I never blame the politicians for wanting it a two-way say-so one bit.

Well, I sent in the drinks, called for the Daimler and sat on dove-colored corduroy for fifty minutes counting snowflakes before Moon showed up. He got in, settled himself under the rug and said, "The Tombs." I lifted the hand phone and said, "The Tombs," and Muddy jerked his head and away we glided for the Tombs.

The clam act was still in order so far as any vital information was concerned, and the run downtown was conversationally confined by Moon to some things he wanted me to attend to. He wanted enough duds shifted from *Coquilla* to *Trade Wind* for a couple of weeks' cruise to Tortuagas, which had been Myron Jettwick's island in the Caribbean and which was now his sister's. Yes, we were going on *Trade Wind*. No, Miss Jettwick knew nothing about it as yet, nor did her yacht, nor did anyone other than Moon and Seward and me.

When we returned from the Tombs I was to telephone all the city desks and inform the editors of *Trade Wind*'s proposed departure. Any move on the part of the murder yacht would be front-page news. Moon specified that the newspapers were to be given the hour of sailing. It would be at five o'clock on the following afternoon.

Miss Jettwick's guests were also to be listed for the press: Mrs. Harriet Schuyler, Elizabeth Schuyler, Moon, myself, Mrs. Helen Jettwick, and Bruce Jettwick. Yes, Bruce. District Attorney Seward would by now have informed the police reporters that Bruce was to be released.

I pointed out that all this was just dandy, and that the city editors would love it, especially if any of the parties involved balked. None, Moon said, going Disraeli, would balk.

How Moon had worked Bruce's release from the holdover was something he obviously preferred to keep under shroud among Seward and McGilvray and himself, and just how strong the leverage was that Moon employed didn't come out until the fireworks had banged and damped and friend trigger-squeezer was headed for his last warm-up.

The official pap to be ladled to an avid public was that the district attorney's office was satisfied that the murder of Jeffry Smith was a direct outcome of the Jettwick case, and that, as Bruce Jettwick could neither have committed nor engineered same from the Tombs, his detention for investigation terminated automatically and he would be released into the custody of his attorney, Mr. Wallace Emberry, who would produce Bruce Jettwick as a material witness when the case came to trial. Important developments trembled on the brink, as per usual, of occurring soon.

Emberry was waiting for us at the Tombs and, the formal odds and ends having been well-oiled through, Bruce became a technically free man again.

The four of us piled into the Daimler after press pictures showing Bruce shaking hands with Emberry, Bruce shaking hands with Moon, Emberry shaking hands with Moon, and me shaking hands with Muddy, just for the hell of it, as Bruce stepped into the car.

Emberry did some polite anglicized fishing on the run uptown trying to hook just how Moon had worked it, and Moon told him nothing at great length and just as politely, while Bruce sat wrapped in the expression of a one-year-old shaking his first pink celluloid rattle.

The fatted calf waiting for us on *Trade Wind* was a canapé spread and champagne at which I found myself the Answer Man to a broadside of questions from Mrs. Schuyler, Helen Jettwick, Elizabeth, and Bruce. Moon had gathered up Miss Jettwick, Emberry, and McRoss and had gone with them into the library to confer.

Well, I ate and drank and answered questions for half an hour, and marveled at the glossy enamel with which nice people can coat their true feelings. Nobody had to be a star-gazer to see that Elizabeth was doing a Hoover-Dam job to keep from spilling her happiness over at seeing Bruce, and ditto with him, and his mother's fingers held the stem of a champagne glass while they were aching to touch some part of him just to be sure he was there.

As for Mrs. Schuyler, you could sense her looking around for ice picks to sink in Bruce, in a nice way of course, to bust up the reunited love feast. I thought then that Moon would have some job in persuading her to be among those present on the Caribbean cruise as she would surely realize, and none quicker, that even ice picks couldn't combat a star-dusted deck, spiced Gulf Stream air, lush palm trees, and a total oblivion to sticky burrs, mosquitoes, flying cockroaches, and a therapeutic caliber of heat.

I was wrong. When the conference broke up in the library and Miss Jettwick issued her invitation, Mrs. Schuyler said that she and Elizabeth would be delighted to accept, and her voice was soft about it, too, even though her eyes were flint.

McRoss was not to be with us. He was going to stay in New York with Emberry and keep right on helping to wind up Myron Jettwick's estate. In my madness, this made me feel that the cruise would turn out to be a simple picnic party after all, what with First Murderer McRoss off the yacht, and I planned to idle the hours away on the brochure I'm writing on "House Specials" or "Bar Tricks Exposed."

Emberry left; we all said good night; we went below. It was half past one. I got busy on phoning the newspapers as per Moon's instructions, and Moon got ready for bed. This was attended to and I'd just settled comfortably under the covers when Moon called me into the bedroom and said:

"Bert, look at this."

It was his copy of *A High Wind in Jamaica* and he handed it to me opened at pages 108-109. Some of the words on page 109 were heavily underlined in pencil, and the two paragraphs that had been marked read:

> *"Remember," Jonsen went on over his shoulder while he searched, "money cannot recall life, nor in the least avail you when you are dead. If you regard your life in the least, at once acquaint me with the hiding place, and your life shall be safe."*
>
> *Marpole's only reply was again to invoke the thought of his wife and children (he was, as a matter of fact, a widower: and his only relative, a niece, would be the better off by his death to the tune of some ten thousand pounds)*

The wallop packed in the message didn't register until I'd repeated the underlined words aloud: *If you regard your life in the least, be off.* You can be superior to threat notes and call them as corny as you like, but wait until you get one. No one knows the statistics on the number issued per year but it's a safe bet that if the government were to put a ten-cent tax on each the national debt would lose a limb. Moon pretends to be very pooh-pooh when he gets one, but they worry and annoy him inside just as much as they do anyone else.

I said that as threat notes go this number was pretty clever, what with the only thing that could be analyzed being the lead marks of the pencil, and that being impossible except for a wizard, and who ever heard anyhow of going up to suspect after suspect and saying:

"Lend me your pencil because—" Which was where Moon shut me up.

He seemed to be very smug and satisfied about the business and said that things were beginning to work, and told me to telephone Jimmy Singer, please, and tell him if he'd located the woman to go ahead as planned. Then he helped himself to some Moreton Bay chestnuts and started cracking them, while staring far, far away through solids such as walls and bulkheads and me and furniture, which was his way of indicating that the interview was closed and kindly shut the bedroom door.

Early in the game, when I first started working for him, Moon said that no matter how confidential my job was there would be moments when he'd lapse into reserves. He said it wasn't any reflection on myself as a lid for secrets, but rather on my erstwhile profession.

He considers bartenders as chronic gossips, claiming that they not only have to take in all the heartaches and local scandals that are handed them across the bar, but also get in the habit of dishing it out. Even if they don't dish he insists that whatever goes into their ears gets printed on their faces whether it comes out of their mouths or stays buttoned up. He's right.

I went to the small switchboard in the coatroom and plugged through to Jimmy Singer's flat. I said when he came to the phone, "If you've located a mouse, known to me only as Madame X, Moon wants you to go ahead as planned," and he said, "Okay, sonny boy," and hung up.

I returned to my lonely cot, crossing my fingers in the deep hope that it would stay lonely and not be a repetition of the previous night, and turned in.

SEVENTEEN

OPENING THE BLACK BOX

The cot stayed perfectly lonely, and maybe that sound night's sleep didn't feel good. It felt good until six o'clock in the morning when some wheezings, puffings, shouts and whistles announced the arrival alongside *Trade Wind* of the Messrs. Seward and McGilvray, the harbor police, a boatload of suspicious, irritable, and puzzled reporters and cameramen, and again the tug from the Manhattan Underseas Contracting Company and a bright good morning to them all.

The snow had stopped and, even though the sky was still black, you could smell through the open porthole that when day broke the river would have a Bon-Ami glint. A cheery hand-wave to District Attorney Seward in his police launch brought a grin, whereas a formal bow to Assistant Police Commissioner McGilvray only further dirtied the look he was already sending toward my head.

The needle stingings of a shower inspired me into a rendition of *Did Your Mother Come from Ireland?* and I managed to get as far as kissing the blarney when Moon opened the bathroom door, looked pained and said:

"No, Bert, Mother didn't."

He started to shave. Then he showered, and I shaved and ordered melon, rolls, and coffee, and dressed in a pretty good Bond Street number which was a tweed on the conservative side even if Moon did suggest you could play games on its checks. A silk tie of regimental stripes topped the works off nicely, and Moon said, "Oh, God," when he came in for breakfast, but I knew he was only ribbing.

We enlarged on breakfast in the dining saloon where everybody had collected shortly after seven, the diving outfit, police, and reporters having made of sleep but a hollow mockery and sham. I said this in just so many words to Elizabeth, who was seated beside me, and she said:

"Nice going, Mr. Stanley. Do you know any others?"

Then she smiled in that hazy way which is so indigenous to half-wits and young lovers.

In fact, for the first time in forty-eight hours the general atmosphere was restful and there wasn't so much tension or barbed nerves. Maybe the morning had something to do with it, because the eastern sky through the ports was a clear grenadine pink. Miss Jettwick had asked Seward and McGilvray to join us, and they had, and Sourpuss McGilvray melted noticeably under some first-rate creamed finnan haddock and popovers that could, when crushed, be put through a needle's eye, or let us settle on a wedding ring in the interests of bare truth.

Miss Jettwick had also telephoned to Emberry about the diving outfit and general doings alongside. He showed up toward eight, shaved and lavender-watered to within an inch, and in time for a final round of coffee. This was barely under his braces when Seward's secretary, Fade-out Wilbur, materialized in the dining-saloon doorway. Under his trembling arm, and dripping, was the black steel box.

I thought I knew then why Moon had had Harry Lochbittern throw it back into the river: so that he could watch some reactions when it was again produced. I looked around for a couple myself and was sorry to find that outside of three the general attitude was one of well-well-look-what's-here. The three were Seward and McGilvray and Mrs. Schuyler. Seward smiled in a knifelike way and glanced at Moon. McGilvray froze sour again. Mrs. Schuyler came across fine by turning an ash-white and drinking a glass of water in a manner that left fifty percent of it cutting channels in her dress.

Seward had Moon's idea about getting reactions, too, because he said that the box would be opened right then and there, with Miss Jettwick's permission, and that she and Mr. Emberry could both be witnesses to the fact that none of the estate's papers were harmed or tampered with by his office although he reserved the right to abstract such ones as he, or Assistant Police Commission McGilvray, might care to impound as evidence.

This eyewash went down all right, and a steward cleared the table while Mouse Wilbur slid off to fetch the department's lock expert. He was right outside on the landing stage, because McGilvray had suspected all along that the steel box was what Moon had sent the diver fishing for the day before.

There was something admirable in the way that Mrs. Schuyler pulled herself together. She couldn't take her eyes away from the box while the expert worked on its lock, but the old burgher blood in her kept a smile of polite interest on her lips and stopped some shivers going through her from showing too much on the outside.

It took forty minutes for the department expert to do what Harry Lochbittern had done in twenty. Wilbur had his limp-leather loose-leaf notebook and pointed pencils ready. As each paper was taken from the box, Seward or McGilvray examined it, had Emberry check it, then Wilbur would stop poising his pencil and flick down what it was. As a matter of fact there weren't many papers, not over fifteen in all, and when the last one was set aside both Seward and McGilvray decided that none was of any value to their case, and turned the lot of them, plus steel box, over to Emberry.

That was when Spider McRoss sounded off.

"Odd," he said. "It's really very odd."

"What is very odd?" McGilvray asked him heavily.

"I rather expected some papers would be there which seem to be missing, Mr. Commissioner."

"Dealing with what?"

"Dealing with Mr. Jettwick's last real-estate project. I've an unconfirmed impression that it revolved around Staten Island. Perhaps you could confirm that, Mrs. Schuyler?"

"In what fashion, Mr. McRoss?"

"I thought that you were interested in the project, too."

"Yes?"

"Well?"

"Well what, Mr. McRoss?"

"Why, shouldn't there be some records, some documentary plans or agreements? I had expected that Mr. Jettwick would have had some in that box, with the rest of his more strictly private papers."

"It would seem that he had not."

"Perhaps," Moon said, "the papers which you feel are missing are somewhere else, Mr. McRoss. Perhaps at his office?"

"Mr. Jettwick had no office."

"Then at his apartment? Or possibly somewhere aboard this yacht?"

Moon was planting some capsules of TNT. I was sure of that, if not just why. I remembered the papers he'd left in the manila envelope in the office safe over at the Manning. His expression was very choirboy and bland, but I knew it was stuffed with canary birds just the same.

EIGHTEEN

THE UNEXPECTED GUEST

Trade Wind's departure from the landing stage of Wharf House was a replica in miniature of any sailing whoop-la'd by *Queen Mary*, and not so miniature at that. Among those present for purposes of bon voyage were: Seward and Fantom Wilbur, Old-lavender Emberry, Poison McRoss, Lettice Laceheart of the *Daily Review*, newsreel cameramen from World Movietone and Globe News, Ltd., the *Press*, most of the two thousand residents of Wharf House either cluttering the landing stage or pushing the panes out of their river-view windows, and many, many casual bystanders who didn't want to be in the way but who did so want to see the fire. It took most of the lads from the local precinct station to keep them safe for the future and on dry land.

The clans started gathering toward four o'clock, and by four-thirty Miss Jettwick came up to us where we were standing near the gangplank on the main deck, and said to Moon:

"Must we wait? Can't we leave now and avoid this? Why wait until five?"

"We are waiting for a guest, Miss Jettwick."

"But everyone's aboard. I hate good-bys under any circumstances, and I've said good-by at length to Wallace Emberry, Mr. McRoss, District Attorney Seward, and Commissioner McGilvray; I've said it at such length that my jaw is becoming strained. That columnist, Miss Laceheart, already has interviewed Bruce and Elizabeth into matrimony and Mrs. Schuyler into apoplexy—Really, Mr. Moon, what other guest?"

"I believe you saw Mrs. Bettling at Santa Monica after that business about her daughter, Eunice, last year. I wonder whether she told you that there was some heathen and some Chinee in me?"

"In the sense that your ways are strange? Yes, as a matter of fact she did. All right. You don't want me to question you. You don't want us to sail until five. Selah! I haven't the faintest idea what that means, but it seems to represent a period mark among some of our Los Angeles cults."

"Thank you, Miss Jettwick. One thing."

"Yes?"

"Could you inconspicuously disentangle Miss Lettice Laceheart from our young romantics, and suggest that if she were to join me on deck she might be given an exclusive?"

"An exclusive story?"

"That's right."

"Leave it to me."

"Just how good are you as a police dog?"

"Perfect, if you eliminate jumping over fences."

"Then here's something else. In about ten or fifteen minutes Mr. Stanley, a nameless woman, Miss Laceheart, and myself will attempt to seclude ourselves in the library. A minute or so before sailing, Miss Laceheart will leave and go ashore. Could you guard us during that interview? Could you see that at no time we are interrupted or disturbed?"

"Yes. Anything else?"

"Nothing else, Miss Jettwick."

"All right, Mr. Moon."

Miss Jettwick left and Moon said:

"When Lettice Laceheart joins us, Bert, please keep an eye on the landing stage for Jimmy Singer. He will have a woman with him and will bring her on deck. If your necktie doesn't stun her into immediate submission, turn on the rest of your charms and get her into the library so fast that she has time neither to see nor to be seen. Miss Laceheart and I will follow."

Miss Laceheart still looked like a leopard without its stuffings when she hustled out on deck and up to Moon. She was an exceedingly hail-fellow-well-met sort of woman and you found yourself instinctively ducking from slaps on the back.

"Hello, hello, hello," she said to Moon, "I hear you've something for me."

"Bringing scoops to your column is like carrying coals to Newcastle, Miss Laceheart," Moon said, turning on the good old F.F.V. gloss.

"You sweet Southern man, you, let's cut the camellias and have a few brass tacks."

"First, conditions."

"Such as?"

"You are going to reserve the coming interview for your column in the morning editions and not release it as press news for tonight."

"Do I look like a zany?"

"Far from it, Miss Laceheart. You look like a leopard."

"Now *stop*! Of course I'll reserve it."

"It will get you into trouble with your editor as the interview will be of a front-page variety, but you will explain to him that you would not have had it without the condition of withholding it until morning."

"This is beginning to sound like something."

"It is. Another condition, your role will be a passive one. I shall do all the talking. Your angle will be that of a sympathetic spectator, and the report in your column will be played up in your accustomed, and inimitable, heart-interest manner. Agreed?"

"Agreed. Who's the interview with?"

"A woman whose name you will know when you are introduced to her in the library."

"Psst!" I said to Moon. "Psst! Pssst!"

"I deduce from the noises that Mr. Stanley is making that she is coming on board now."

She was. Jimmy Singer was piloting her through the mob on the landing stage, and even in all that mess she looked like a good hot number, in a hammered iron way. Jimmy shot her along the gangplank and up to me, and said to her, "Clark Gable Stanley will take you to Mr. Moon right away."

"Goody," she said in a voice fresh out of the glowing forge.

Well, Jimmy gave me one of those things it pleases him to think of as a kittenish look, dropped her arm and beat it, and I hooked her arm and started swinging her along.

"Where to, handsome?" she said, and I said, "Ever read a book, thunderbolt?" and she said, "What is a book?" and I said, "You'll see lots of them right now," and buried the persiflage, hefted her into the library and shut the door.

Moon opened it right away again and let in Miss Laceheart, then closed it, and said to Lady Vulcan, "I believe you have a grievance, Mrs. Smith? This is my secretary, Mr. Bert Stanley, and Miss Lettice Laceheart of the *Daily Review*"

Miss Laceheart let out a squeal. "Not—not Mrs. *Jeffry* Smith? The wife of the man who was bumped—Oh, my dear child, *do* forgive me! Your grief—"

"You can tie a can on my grief. I'm here on business."

Moon firmly grabbed the throttle.

"Mrs. Smith, I understand from Mr. Singer that the situation is this. He found you at your hotel last night after the sudden demise of your husband and suggested that if you changed your hotel you would not be inconvenienced by the police who, in turn, might locate you for questioning. I doubt strongly whether they could have. They do not quite have all of Mr. Singer's facilities."

"Singer did. He told me Jeff was all set to take a powder."

"Precisely, utilizing the ten-thousand-dollar reward I had offered."

"Which should now be mine, by rights."

"Possibly, Mrs. Smith, it shall be yours."

"Jeff filled his part of the bargain. He got shot for it."

"He was shot, unfortunately, before he had given me any information whatever."

"That's what you say."

"It is also what you will have to believe. I had Mr. Singer bring you to me to make you this proposition: tell me what your husband was on the point of disclosing when he died, and the ten thousand will be yours."

"I don't know."

"I was afraid of that."

"Jeff kept a lot of stuff from me. He had funny ideas about women."

"I am told that you married him shortly after he acted as correspondent in the divorce case between Myron and Helen Jettwick?"

"That's right."

"I think that the information he was about to sell me concerns that general period. My proposition is this, Mrs. Smith. Accompany us on this cruise. During it I shall attempt to spur your memory as to every small detail you recall of the early years of your marriage, your memory of every reference which your husband may have made to you that touched on the Jettwick divorce, of everything Mrs. Jettwick may have told your husband regarding the jewel thefts on the *Leviathan*, and any reference, no matte how slight, to Senator Blackman and his wife."

"Suppose I can't remember anything important, Mr. Moon?"

"I am satisfied to make a bargain with you right now. If you do your part honestly, and help me with every remembrance that can be brought back, I will give you the ten thousand dollars whether your information proves to be important or not. I am satisfied that it will. Well, Mrs. Smith?"

"It's a deal. I'd be a dimwit if it wasn't."

"Thank you. Miss Laceheart, there is your story. I suggest you play it from the angle of the grief-stricken widow who is racking her brains even through cruel heartache to remember the vital clue which her husband was about to impart when he was brutally shot; the clue that will lead us to his murderer."

"I'll probably get canned for holding this stuff back, but it's worth it."

"You are holding it back under compulsion of your promise to me. Also, please radio a complete copy of the item as it appears in your column to our operator on board. He will incorporate it in the ship's news."

I began to get it right then. People believe what they see in print. Moon wanted somebody on board to read that item and, because it had been printed in a New York newspaper, it would be accepted as a fact. The edges were still hazy, but Moon stopped further cogitations by saying to Miss Laceheart:

"We are about to cast off and I advise you to go ashore and—vanish."

She did, almost dropping her spots in her hurry, and I said to Moon:

"Seward and McGilvray are going to be too pleased for words about all this."

"By tomorrow morning, Bert, we shall be far beyond their jurisdiction."

"What about the coast guard? I understand they float?"

"We are committing no felony. Mrs. Smith is accompanying us of her own free will. She will inform the press of that fact by radio-telephone tomorrow. I know of no precedent for removing on the high seas a person who is wanted for simple questioning. The very thought is an absurdity."

"Hey, listen, you two," Mrs. Smith said. "What about clothes? What am I supposed to do? Morning-noon-and-night in these?"

"I dare say Miss Schuyler or Mrs. Jettwick will be glad to help you out. You are about their size. Naturally, when you return with the ten thousand dollars, you can buy all the clothes you like."

"You've got some warm ideas, Mr. Moon. My bet is that you're a bachelor."

"I am, shall we say, for the time being? There is one thing which you must understand, Mrs. Smith. I speak for your own safety, and I speak seriously. Mr. Stanley is not only my secretary; he is an efficient bodyguard. That is, in any situation which does not involve a porthole. You will be forced to put up with a close attendance on his part both on the run down and during our stay at Tortuagas. I trust you will be freed from this attention on the run back North as I expect that the case will be closed before we leave the island. My sympathies."

Baby Ironside's pretty violet-colored eyes took a round-trip ticket starting from my head and said, "Don't waste them on me, Mr. Moon. Give them to him."

I thought I was shivering because I suddenly realized what Moon really wanted her on board for. The papers from the black steel box which he'd packed at the Manning weren't enough to prove his case. He had to force the killer's hand by setting a trap, and Jeffry Smith's happy relict was to be the bait.

But I wasn't shivering. It was *Trade Wind*, and we moved over to the starboard portholes and stared out. The gangplank had been lowered, and water showed and widened along *Trade Wind*'s side. You could see

Emberry and McRoss and Seward and McGilvray lined up with the mob on the landing stage, and I waved a kiss to McGilvray that almost rocked him into the drink.

Then *Trade Wind*'s nose swung out, her whistle blew and her turbines throbbed her gently forward into the chop.

NINETEEN

ABSENCE OF BLOOD AND THUNDER

Hatteras, Charleston, Savannah, Jacksonville Beach, the hard sands of Daytona, Miami Beach with its buildings sticking up like gaunt white fingers, Key West, all were dropped astern and we were due to raise Tortuagas toward evening. Not being a seventh son and having no facility with tea leaves whatever, even if my grandmother had been an O'Michael of Kilkenny, there was no way of knowing the terrible sort of hell that Tortuagas was due to raise with us.

I had tried on the run down, during a lull in my bodyguard act over Mrs. Smith, to pry Moon loose from the answers to several key questions which struck me as summing up the case, and being pertinent as all get-out.

Who, I asked him, had packed down the snow on *Trade Wind*'s small aft-deck, leaving footprints and the icy patch where "who" had stood for some time and looked in through the open porthole. And why?

Could a woman as well as a man have imitated the general tones of Myron Jettwick's voice when Bruce had been summoned by the boat telephone to his uncle's quarters in order to place Bruce on the scene of the crime? I pointed out that some waterfront packets I'd faced across the bar at Harrigan's Tavern had had voices like stevedores, and vice versa, so what?

When had the bottle of Jamaica rum been stolen from *Trade Wind*'s stores: the bottle which the man with the white dress shirt front had given to Terrence, the steward on deck watch, in order to grease him into a fade-out? When had the sapucaia nuts been stolen from Bruce's pocket, and how?

Who had lifted the black steel box from behind the books of botany, and when had it been tossed over the side?

Who were the two punks in the rowboat who had been grappling for that box, or who had hired them?

How had Mr. Who known that Jeffry Smith had made a date to meet us in that bar on Fifty-fourth Street? When had the threat note been underlined in Moon's copy of *A High Wind in Jamaica*?

Had the ex-wife of Senator Blackman lied when she claimed she had not seen Myron Jettwick again after his call at the Waldorf?

What was the true answer to Mrs. Schuyler's hat: the fact that it had been on her head at six-thirty in the a.m.?

Moon answered me by asking a question. Which probable motive struck my fancy? There were three: profit, revenge, and fear. Just those three shells, he said, and under one of them would be the pea, so I saw he was only going to play games and that any further prying at the moment would be a waste of breath.

This happened on the third day out and Moon was sitting on the main deck wearing, with white linens, a huge straw farmer's hat. He thinks getting sunburned is silly and always uses my painful initial lobster stages in tanning as proof of his point. He got rid of me by asking me to call up Emberry on the radio-telephone and find out what papers, if any, had turned up in Myron Jettwick's apartment that might have a bearing on the Staten-Island-project end of the investigation.

Kenny Mattson, *Trade Wind*'s radio operator, was an agreeable kid, very plump and addicted to penny ante and to whistling off key. He put me through to Emberry's apartment in New York City, which was a duplex and terraced affair complete with four exposures and four views. Miss Jettwick had told me about it.

A man's voice said, "Hello?"

I said, "Hello."

That being got over with we attacked business.

"Mr. Wallace Emberry, please. Bert Stanley speaking."

"This is Plymouth, Mr. Emberry's man, sir. Mr. Emberry is not at home."

"Is he over at Mr. Myron Jettwick's apartment?"

"No, sir. Mr. Emberry is at Cotswold."

"At what?"

"Cotswold, sir. His estate on the north shore of Long Island."

"What's the number?"

Plymouth gave it to me, and I gave it to Kenny Mattson, who put it through, and Emberry answered the call himself. I told him what Moon wanted.

"Yes, Mr. Stanley, I have."

His voice sounded pale and upset, if you can imagine a voice doing anything like that. He said he had been on the point of calling *Trade Wind* up and telling Moon all about it. He and McRoss had continued their search after papers in Jettwick's apartment that morning, and a memorandum had been found between the leaves of a book on the cultivation of artichokes. The memorandum obviously referred to a more important document which, it said, was among the papers in the black steel box.

Well, Emberry had gone to his retreat on Long Island where he had transferred the box and the apparently unsignificant contents, but, unless some of the stuff was code, he still could find no paper to which the memo might have referred.

It wasn't that, however, which had made his voice pale and upset. He had been robbed. Someone had broken into Cotswold and had lifted a sterling silver tea service, and, apart from the intrinsic loss, there was the sentimental one as well. The tea service had belonged to his grandmother. He had gotten in touch with the state police, but, outside of covering the known fences and pawnshops, I knew, he said, what that meant.

From my vague knowledge of Emberry's origin the sentimental angle was just so much prize beef on the hoof, as the height of his grandmother's elegance in tea services probably never reached beyond an earthenware pot marked "Souvenir of St. Louis' World Fair." So I said dear-dear and my-my and promised to tell Moon all about the memorandum and the theft, then sent my regards to Poison McRoss, and was about to ring off when he stopped me and wanted to know whether Mrs. Smith had been able to remember anything of importance as yet. I said no, but she was trembling on the brink, and said good-by.

I reported this riffle of useless information to Moon, but the theft of the tea service seemed to interest him and he said, "Thank you, Bert," and waved a smoke screen about his person which meant that he wanted to be alone.

My charge was sun-tanning herself on deck up in the bows so I went within eyesight of her and sat down to add a paragraph to my brochure as I thought she was safely asleep. She was beside me before I could put a period after the title to the paragraph "House Specials So What."

She twisted her neck over my shoulder.

"Often I have wondered about house specials, Mr. Stanley. How come the cash customers don't get wise to the fact that they're tea?"

Because, I told her, they are not tea: they're the accumulated rinsings of the liquor and cordial bottles before the bottles are so wastefully broken because of the ABC law. These rinsings are then bottled and given a fancy name which no liquid gourmet ever heard of in his life. They have plenty of flavor but no kick, and whatever wren in the clip joint the purchasing sucker is honoring at six bits a drink can pack them away all night and still keep her wits about her, even if she does lose her sense of taste. The profit to the house being just one hundred percent.

She poured sun-tan oil on my back and started to rub it in. Suppose, she said, the sucker reaches over and takes a drink of the special himself? Sometimes, I told her, they do, and if they like the backwash of a week's rinsings and order one for themselves the waiter signals the bartender who then spikes the special with a shot of gin. This cuts down on the profit a little, but mellows the sucker into the proper state of putty for being shortchanged and totally gypped.

Well, all that had been two days before we were due to raise Tortuagas, and, so help me, not another thing had happened on the trip. The wireless-news' item of Lettice Laceheart's scoop on Mrs. Smith had apparently been received by all on board without an eyelash being batted, and Mrs. Smith herself had been received in the same manner. The girls couldn't have been nicer to her if she'd been lightly dusted over with powdered arsenic; very formal and very right whenever they spoke to her, and most kind about lending her their duds to wear, but you could tell that Mrs. Smith got it and felt it, too.

The only squawk about Mrs. Smith's having joined the party had come in a radio from McGilvray to Moon saying, under quotes: "A wise man will not reprove a fool," and Moon had made a spill of the message and dropped it over the side. He said it was a Chinese proverb and he hadn't thought McGilvray had had it in him, which kept it still in the original Chinese to me.

As for the lovebirds, Elizabeth might just as well have been in a cage, her mother being the cage, because there wasn't a minute when Mrs. Schuyler wasn't on hand whenever Bruce was near by and awake.

Not that this absence of blood and thunder made for peace; on the contrary, it was like the slow building up of an invisible pressure within sealed walls with the time shortly due when the whole works were to burst, and our first sight of Tortuagas came as a relief.

We raised the island just at twilight on the evening of *Trade Wind*'s fifth day out, and District Attorney Seward was waiting for us on the dock.

TWENTY

TO SHOOT A SPARROW DOWN

Long shadows of the royal palms with which Myron Jettwick had landscaped the harbor's fringe of Tortuagas were like indigo pencils on copper sand in that swift tropical descent of the setting sun. Grouped on the dock around Seward as *Trade Wind* gently nosed her way along-side were several white-jacketed black boys from the house, and a Mr. Warrenby Dorset who served, Miss Jettwick told us, as a year-round major-domo on the island.

Moon called down to Seward from the starboard rail, where he was standing with the rest of us.

"I might have known you'd be here."

Seward grinned up.

"I realized it was just an oversight on Miss Jettwick's part, my not having been asked."

"Did you bring anybody else?"

"No, I'm all."

"How did you get here?"

"I flew down yesterday."

"Here?"

"No, to Key West, and chartered a boat to bring me over. Quite a place you have here, Miss Jettwick."

"Is it? That's nice."

You could see that Miss Jettwick felt a sudden stab of fear in spite of these pleasantries. It was a cinch she was figuring that only one sane reason could have brought Seward down from New York: to make an arrest.

She glanced at Bruce, who was standing beside her, and his face was undoubtedly pale under the tan he'd coated it with on the way down. Helen Jettwick had a strained look in her eyes, too, while Mrs. Schuyler's normally well-trained features had frozen into a snow face from the moment when she had identified Seward on the dock.

Elizabeth managed to keep on looking sophisticated, if none too happy, and Mrs. Smith just gave Seward the once-over as she did with anybody in pants.

"How do you do, Miss Jettwick?" Dorset called up. "I'm Warrenby Dorset. Your brother frequently spoke about you—beastly thing, his death. I'd like to welcome you to Tortuagas."

"Thank you, Mr. Dorset. Myron often spoke to me of you, too."

The landing ladder was lowered and we went ashore and followed a path bordered with hedges of bougainvillea that wound through a lush jungle of bamboo trees and coconut palms with some flame trees brightening the gloom. The house itself was a natural for a night club, and of the Spanish type which they knock together so well at Palm Beach and practically nowhere else, including Spain.

A large inner patio had a pool in its center, while galleries surrounded three of its sides, with latticed doors opening into bedrooms. There were outside staircases of Spanish tile and wrought-iron work going up to the gallery.

Miss Jettwick left it to Warrenby Dorset to bed us down, and only specified that Helen Jettwick's room should adjoin hers. Dorset had arranged dinner for half past eight so we scattered behind our black boys to go to our rooms and bathe and dress.

Moon had talked to Dorset, with the result that Moon and I and Mrs. Smith and Seward were lined up along the southern gallery in the order named. Moon splashed happily in the tub of our connecting bathroom while I shaved, and I asked him when his capsules of TNT were scheduled to pop off, and he asked me for God's sake not to wear a white mess jacket, so I put on a white mess jacket with a cummerbund of black silk because Mrs. Smith had said if there ever was a physique for one it was mine. I told Moon this, and he submerged in the tub and blew bubbles until I hauled him up.

Dinner was a good enough meal, with pompano for an entree and hot stone crabs with melted butter as a main course, all sluiced down by a light German wine. Brother Dorset sat himself beside Miss Jettwick and spanked the conversation with a verbal Cook's tour of Tortuagas which was, he said, roughly fifteen square miles in area, was densely impenetrable over most of its surface, but did contain a citrus grove of a size and productivity that had made the island not alone self-supporting but capable of showing a profit as well.

Coffee was served in the patio, and it was fun to watch the sweet job Seward made of herding Mrs. Smith over into a corner where the shrubs were densest. They sat there, deep in the shadows, and I was thinking of strolling over there myself when Moon said he'd like me to get my notebook and join Helen Jettwick and Miss Jettwick and himself in Miss Jettwick's room.

Moon started right in as soon as I got there and said, "Mrs. Jettwick, the time has come when I shall have to revive some memories that will be painful to you."

"About my marriage to Myron?"

"Even further back than that; say, from the time when you left your home in Vermont and came to the city."

Helen Jettwick was, she told us, the daughter of a good New England family with a lieutenant governor, a bishop, and a wealth of lesser fry on its tree. Her father had been a Methodist minister with an almost literal belief in the heating apparatus of hell, which was why she had gone to New York, to escape, and to marry Myron's younger brother Alfred.

"How did you happen to meet Alfred Jettwick?"

"Myron introduced me to him."

Miss Jettwick drew her breath in sharply and said, "Myron? You knew Myron first?"

"Yes. Didn't he ever tell you? His original interests in real estate were around Greenwich Village, in the smallest sort of a way, of course. He had a rental agency for the cheaper type of lodgings, and I happened to go to it when I was looking about for a place to stay. We became friends. He took me out frequently to dinner, and sometimes to a concert afterwards."

"Myron? Well!" Miss Jettwick continued to be amazed. "I never was aware of his interest in music."

"He had none, really. I was a lonely sort of dreamy little fool in those days, and felt terribly grateful for the least sort of attention from anybody. There was an assured sort of kindliness about Myron that I liked. About a month after we had met each other he took me to an art students' dance at Webster Hall, and it was there that he introduced me to Alfred."

Helen Jettwick looked speculatively at her sister-in-law. "I wonder whether you realized how different both of them were?"

"Of course I realized, Helen. They were completely different, in looks and in everything else."

Helen Jettwick's smile fanned a chill along my spine, not one of fright, but the kind you sometimes get when you're in church and thinking of this and that and look up and see the lips on the picture of a madonna.

"After I met Alfred there wasn't anyone else on earth but Alfred. We neither of us had any doubt from that first moment when we danced together. Nothing could have kept us apart, and nothing did."

"And Myron?" Moon said, with his foot jammed hard on the soft pedal.

Helen Jettwick turned again to Miss Jettwick, looking for understanding. She just sat there thinking back on things for a moment, while palm fronds clashed their soft clatter out beyond the gallery, and you could hear voices from the patio below. Mrs. Schuyler's voice was very plain, and she was saying:

"No, Elizabeth, I shall not have you strolling down to the dock with Bruce or any place else. That pathway on the way up was cluttered with tarantulas, blue lizards, and that ghastly iguana. Either continue your backgammon or else go to bed."

That settled that, and Helen Jettwick picked up the thread:

"Myron was in love with me, but he hadn't realized it until he saw me dancing with Alfred. He told me that, one night in Africa."

You could almost see the effort it took her to control herself at some memory before she could go on.

"Myron proposed to me. I think it was about two weeks after the dance, and I didn't learn until years later how deeply my refusal had hurt him. Hurt is such a weak word for what he felt, because it never left him, but just took root and rankled and festered inside of him while he went right on loving me and wanting me more and more. Does it seem impossible to you that a man could feel like that?"

"No," Moon said, "it doesn't."

He picked out some of the nastier, but terribly human, stuff that the cops would come across almost in their daily work: youngsters of the age that Myron Jettwick had been, bashing their girls' heads loose with tire tools, giving them multiple wounds with a knife or blasting them with a pepper grinder when the girls had turned them down. A man scorned, he said, was just as lethal as a woman scorned, possibly because a lot of men have a lot of woman in them, and that was one of the ways it cropped out.

"It was there all the time," Helen Jettwick went on. "It was there after Alfred and I were married, only Myron hid it awfully well. I think that he liked to torture himself with it, in the sense of a mental flagellation, because he couldn't have been kinder to Alfred and me whenever we were in actual want or trouble of any financial sort."

She detoured for a minute to give us a picture of her home life with Alfred after the wedding. You got it that young Alfred had had a good baritone of a church-choir variety, plenty of good looks, in contrast to Big Brother Myron's more candid-camera mug, but no dramatic ability whatever.

She and Alfred had lived very happily in a dumpy hovel under the el, mostly on a diet of Italian pastas larded with garlic, and he made what pennies he could by singing in fourth-rate concerts and with choral societies that were formed for their members' own satisfaction and little else.

Both of them had idolized from this mole's viewpoint Brother Myron's grandiose plans and dreams, which were shortly to start bringing home the bacon as facts.

"I think it really did give Myron a sort of masochistic pleasure to help us out," Helen Jettwick said. "Alfred and I naturally looked on him as some sort of a god, one whom we only had to appeal to and all of our difficulties were smoothed away. There were ten years of that, and Bruce had grown to be a boy of nine, and then Alfred was killed."

A sort of bleached look settled on her face before she went on. Myron had asked her to marry him, right off the bat, and you knew she had agreed to, in order to repay him for his ten years of many kindnesses.

She also had Bruce's future to consider, and had doped it out that the kid would be more secure as Myron's stepson and living under Myron's various roofs than as a nephew getting handouts whenever the flour ran low.

She put it this way:

"It was like something that he had bought after bargaining for with fate for a long time. Myron's getting me to marry him, I mean. I must sound terribly conceited saying all this, but that happens to be the way it was."

"Mr. Moon did not know Myron," Miss Jettwick said incisively, "but I did." She leaned over and pressed one of Helen Jettwick's nervous hands. "You did, too."

How well, it seemed, nobody had ever known until then. You caught the nightmare that had followed her marriage to Myron, so shortly after Alfred's funeral in Vienna; a nightmare made up of knowing that Myron loved her passionately but hated her, too, hated her with a vindictiveness that had made every moment of her life with him a hell. Because she had turned him down. Because he was physically ugly and Alfred hadn't been, and because she had loved Alfred. Because (and this was the hottest because of all) she had married him out of sympathy for the kindnesses he had done, so pervertedly, for her and for Alfred and for Bruce.

Miss Jettwick said:

"He always wanted his revenge, Helen. Even when we were children he would want it whenever he fancied some slight to his pride or couldn't have his own way. He would generally manage to get it."

"It was Myron, of course, who stole the jewelry aboard the *Leviathan*?" Moon said.

Helen Jettwick looked at him curiously. I did, too, as the statement seemed a pretty big rabbit to pull out of anybody's hat. Then I remembered the manila envelope in the safe at the Manning and realized it probably wasn't only full of rabbits, but goldfish bowls and the flags of all nations.

"You know that?" Helen Jettwick said.

"Yes."

"I didn't think of it, not for many years, and then I began to feel positive that nobody else could have hidden the jewels among my things, or would have. It was a certainty, a conviction that came too late."

"And the divorce, Mrs. Jettwick?"

It was then that she started to cry. It was a good downfall but she kept talking right on through it.

"I would have turned," she said, "to a stone for sympathy. The deadest, cheapest, foulest person in the world could have said to me, 'I'm sorry for you,' and I would have clung to him. I did."

"Jeffry Smith?"

"Yes, Jeffry."

"And then?"

"But don't you see? Jeffry had been hired by Myron and paid for doing just that. I can't prove it, but nothing will ever make me believe anything else."

Well, we left them with Miss Jettwick doing the mopping up, and I asked Moon just what new enlightenments he had gleaned from all of that. Strangely enough, he answered me.

"I am now thoroughly convinced that no arguments or pleas on the part of his murderer could have swerved Myron Jettwick from his plan."

"What plan?"

"A plan to blast the world apart, if he had to, in order to shoot a sparrow down."

He couldn't have made things plainer if he'd written me a letter in invisible ink.

TWENTY-ONE
"HE'S IT!"

We turned in shortly after eleven and it was that night, during the narcotic hush of the steaming tropics, that friend killer got busy again and cut another notch in the grip of his gun. Only it wasn't a gun.

There was no wind, and heat from the torrid day still formed a thick blanket on the dead night air. All of the latticed doors opening onto the gallery were left open, and the night became very mute with the only thing you could hear being the splash of water from a fountain in the patio's central pool. It was all very trickle and Spanish and correct, but it sounded like a leaky tap to me.

For Moon suggested, just before he went to sleep, that I stay up. He wanted me to take my gun and my thoughts and camp out all night on a chair beside the lattice door to Mrs. Smith's room. Well, I did just that, pushing the chair under the shadow of a white-flowered vine with a thick sweet odor that would have gone over great at a funeral.

I sat. I didn't smoke, being used to giving it up during vigils of that nature. I contemplated all my thoughts, wondering whether the dead silence and oppressive heat spelled storm as it had that time Moon chased *Coquilla* after some *inocarpus edulis* in the South Sea Islands, they being Tahiti chestnuts and the exclusive property of the natives for all of me; wondering about the memo which Emberry and Snake-eye McRoss had found in the book on artichokes and whether it did refer to some paper which Moon had cached at the Manning, or if the paper were hidden somewhere else.

In Jettwick's apartment? Aboard *Trade Wind* or—I rated a mental kick for not thinking of it before—right here, right on Tortuagas, which was remote enough and private enough, and what else had given Moon the notion of coming down here, otherwise, in the first place?

And then—that's right—I went sound asleep. The eastern sky looked as if it had been hit by a box of ripe raspberries when I woke up. Dew had given me a good chill, and the world seemed queer for the first few seconds while I was trying to shake loose from a bad dream dealing with portholes, rowboats, and blistering socks on the head. Anyone could see pneumonia, rheumatism, and swamp fevers leering out of that humid dawn so I started to stand up and stretch when I heard the noise.

Nothing can freeze you quicker than a strange noise in a world that's dead. It came from Mrs. Smith's room and it sounded like a defect in a bathtub drain, only muted the way trumpets are muted by a coked player in a sugar band. It was a whole lot darker still in that room than it was outside and the thought of silhouetting my physique with all its vital spots in the lattice doorway seemed a bad hunch, so I flattened on the tiles and looked inside.

At first you could see nothing but a thick violet haze and then, over by the room's inner doorway, I saw what looked like a bundle and the bundle seemed to twitch. That was enough to kill the Fenimore Cooper method of advance and I hit the bundle in two leaps and found it was Mrs. Smith. She was not only trussed up, but was very quickly choking to death from a length of fishline that had been wrapped and knotted around her throat.

She was, as has been hinted, a case-hardened baby, which was just as well, as otherwise, another minute or two would have seen her swinging a harp. A penknife took care of the fishline, and there was far too much to do right then to lead her safely through the after-effects of attempted strangulation to go chasing after the bird who had done it.

Anyhow, it seemed reasonable at the moment that said bird was synthetically snoring beneath bedcovers all ready to wake up surprised when the attack or corpse was announced.

Mrs. Smith was conscious after ten minutes of good, honest work, which left me in one of the deepest and most thankful sweats on record, when she croaked in a fool sort of whisper:

"I woke up just as he slid the cord under my neck. Did you get him, Mr. Stanley?"

"No, I didn't. Quit talking for a while."

"Who was it?"

"I don't know. Keep still."

If her, thought I, why not Moon, too? He has an uncanny ability for taking care of himself and hates being worried about, but I lifted Mrs. Smith from the floor just the same, and started to head through the murky haze for the bed when Moon said from the lattice doorway:

"No, Bert, not the bed. There is someone on it already."

I did not drop Mrs. Smith. No matter how many times either she or Moon may claim so, I did not drop Mrs. Smith. His voice, his whisper, had given her a convulsive start, and could I help that?

"Why not," Moon said, "some light?"

He left me to re-collect Mrs. Smith, and went to a wall switch and turned on the ceiling lamp, which was an ormolu nifty patterned after the kind once in vogue aboard Spanish galleons.

McRoss was on the bed.

He had come, I figured, to a very horrible, but fitting, end. A razor blade had slipped from the fingers of his right hand and lay, just beneath them, on the tiled floor. A slash across his throat oozed red, and the setup looked a natural: he'd come down to get the incriminating paper referred to in the memo and to stop Mrs. Smith before she remembered and talked; then he had sliced himself in that fit of remorse which sometimes hits amateur killers directly on top of their crime. I said to Moon:

"He's it, isn't he?"

Moon said, "Yes, Bert. He's it."

It was hours later, after a good deal of messy this and that, that I knew Moon's "it" referred to the goat in the game of tag, and this error in understanding went a long way toward almost losing me my only and valuable skin.

TWENTY-TWO

EARTHQUAKE

Well, Moon told me acidly that Mrs. Smith would revive herself, and this time to let her stay on the floor as it was better for her than being constantly dropped, and he asked me to wake up District Attorney Seward and send him in. Then he wanted me to go down to *Trade Wind*, radio-telephone Wallace Emberry and find out when was the last time he had seen McRoss and if he knew anything in connection with McRoss's having left New York.

I woke Seward and warned him of the surprise waiting for him in the next room, then went down to the patio and took the path for the dock. It was a relief, as it always is, to picture the case as closed, and I daydreamed while stepping along between the bougainvillea hedges of a pleasant run back North, with Mrs. Smith being deeply grateful during moonlight nights on deck for having been saved from a good garroting, even if she should happen to be lame for a couple of days from her own spasmodic exits from my arms.

The dock was deserted. So were *Trade Wind*'s decks and those of *Flamingo*, the small cruiser which Warrenby Dorset used to ferry between the island and Key West.

Kenny Mattson was sound asleep in his bunk, but he woke up with a perfectly natural grouch, put on *espadrillos*, lit a cigarette and went with me into the wireless room. I gave him the news about Mrs. Smith and McRoss, and, being a screwball like most wireless operators, he was cheered almost to pieces at being in the vicinity of attempted murder and violent death. If I missed a detail in describing the horrible scene it certainly wasn't that lad's fault. He even wanted to know the make of the razor blade which wasn't, when I came to think of it, such a dumb question at that.

He had some trouble in raising New York because, he said, of atmospherics, and, when he did get through, he was told that Emberry's apartment didn't answer. He tried the Long Island number, and after ten minutes or so told me that the call was through.

"Mr. Wallace Emberry, please," I said. "Bert Stanley talking."

"Speak a little louder, Mr. Stanley. I'm Emberry. Your voice sounds like a catastrophe in tin pans."

"So does yours, Mr. Emberry. I'm calling about McRoss."

"Yes?"

"He's dead. He committed suicide with a razor blade."

"What? What? God bless my soul! Where? In town?"

"No, down here—Tortuagas."

"But he isn't down there. He's up here."

"No, he isn't, and Moon wanted me to find out from you when you saw him last."

"Last? Why, yesterday morning when we met at Jettwick's apartment. Why on earth did he do it?"

"Remorse."

"He confessed? This bowls me completely over. He left a confession?"

"No, but it's obvious from what he tried to do to Mrs. Smith. He tried to strangle her."

"I can't believe it—McRoss—McRoss of all people!"

"What time did you leave him at Jettwick's apartment yesterday?"

"Early—around ten or eleven in the morning, I think, because Plymouth called for me then and we drove out here to Cotswold."

"That's all you know."

"Yes, and I wish to heavens you'd tell me more."

"Maybe later, Mr. Emberry. Right now I've got to report to Mr. Moon. Good-by."

"Good-by."

Six bells struck, and a very odd-looking sky greeted us when we stepped out on deck, a very odd sky for seven o'clock in the morning. It was like a new copper penny, without a trace of blue.

"Oh, boy!" Kenny Mattson said, taking a look at it. "Maybe it's a tropical storm—wait until I take a look at the glass. Oh, boy!"

He was off for the chartroom and back again in no time with Captain Plummet, who wore a singlet, white-duck pants, boiled-beef skin, and a worried look.

"She's dropping," Kenny said. "Oh, boy, is she falling down!"

Captain Plummet gave him a suet eye, confirmed the fact that we might be in for a bit of weather, then studied the heavens absently while I recounted again, and with several promptings from Kenny Mattson, the doings last night up at the house.

Moon and Seward and Warrenby Dorset came down the path and joined us on the bridge deck by the time I was through. The amenities were negligible, and it turned out that Dorset was going to send *Flamingo* over to Key West with a couple of the black boys. This was at Seward's request, as the inquiry into McRoss's death fell under the jurisdiction of the Florida state authorities, and, what with the climate and everything else, the sooner they hustled over and took a look, the better everything would be.

Flamingo shoved off and we went back to the house, where I put on white linens under the irrepressible delusion that they would be cool. Everybody was up, of course, and in a fine lather of shock and fright and worry even though the general opinion coincided with mine: that McRoss had been the villain and that the case was closed. It was an opinion that neither Seward nor Moon, the rats, made the slightest effort to contradict.

We gathered for breakfast in the patio at eight, and a fine crew we looked, too, because of the excitement and the drenching heat, and with only Mrs. Smith looking chilly whenever she glanced toward me. What air there was filled with why's. Why had Myron Jettwick been killed in the first place? Why this? Why that? Why? Why?

Moon told them, in part, while the women waved palm-leaf fans, and us men mopped at dripping sweat and a couple of worried parakeets chattered about the perilous weather from a flame tree near the table.

The case hinged, Moon said—still shying clear of the word "solution"—on a remark that he had made last night to me: on the fact that Myron Jettwick had been willing to blast the world apart, if he had to, in order to shoot a sparrow down.

Moon said:

"I think we must accept the fact, Miss Jettwick, that your brother Myron was a thoroughly egocentric man. I mean that the slightest thing which affected him personally became of paramount importance, to a point where any means seemed justifiable either to attain that thing or to defend himself against it. Whenever he could do so, however, he preferred to sugar-coat his means to the end."

Moon shifted to Helen Jettwick and said:

"His implacable hatred of you and your son is my case in point." (I settled back and became Patience, because when Moon starts handing out words like egocentric, paramount, and implacable, he's fogging an issue which, while important and true enough in itself, is simply a mask to screen an issue that is more important still. It gave me a hint that all was not well among the Danes and I started to guess. The trouble is, I didn't guess right.) "You were perfectly correct, Mrs. Jettwick, in your reaction to his invitation for the Tortuagas cruise."

"He did want to hurt me through Bruce because Bruce was successful and secure? He did want to tear our life apart again?"

"Yes, but let me make this plain to you. It was acting, but it was such sincere acting that he deceived himself. I refer to the reconciliation angle, the setting of his house in order before he died. They were the sugar-coating of his means to their cruel end. The stroke he suffered from blood pressure unquestionably accented the possibility that death could be close, and he did want, as the Reverend Munster Grant put it, an insurance policy for his soul. Do you see the double feature of his plan?"

"Yes, I think I do. He would save his soul by admitting to me that he himself had done the *Leviathan* thefts in order to brand me as a thief and had arranged the divorce to brand me as a wanton. No, it still isn't clear, Mr. Moon. How could he admit those things publicly without clearing my name? If Bruce, as the Unknown Troubadour, were exposed under such circumstances as my son, he would be thought of as the son of a martyr, a woman who had been bitterly wronged. Surely that wasn't what Myron wanted, was it?"

"No. His plan seems complicated until you reduce it to simple moves. 'A': he had a press release prepared, which he intended to mail to the newspapers on the morning that *Trade Wind* sailed. I have that document in my possession."

"Really?" Seward said coldly.

"Yes. The release mentions the precarious condition of Myron Jettwick's health and his desire to effect a reconciliation with his divorced wife and his nephew so that the short span of life left him may be passed with a sense of amity among them. He states that Mrs. Jettwick and Bruce accepted his invitation for the Caribbean cruise to cement that reconciliation. He does not omit the fact that Bruce is professionally known as Bruce Lane, the Unknown Troubadour. Well, Bruce is prominent enough to be news, and Jettwick stopped right there and left it to the yellower of the sheets to go to their morgues, dig into the past and attend to the rest."

Miss Jettwick said:

"Helen would have combated that release with one of her own, stating that Myron had admitted to her his responsibility for the theft and the divorce."

"Admitted to her, Miss Jettwick, yes. It would be her word against his, and the damage would have been done."

"Then what about his precious soul? How could he squirm validity into its insurance policy if he didn't back her up?"

"That question brings us to move 'B': he had written out a confession as to the thefts and the divorce. It is a detailed confession, explaining his motivation and every move that he made."

"You have it, of course?" Seward said, and a whole lot colder than before.

"Of course. It was kept, he planned to tell Mrs. Jettwick, among his most private papers, papers that would not be examined until after his death. It would offer her complete exoneration and he would have given it to her at once—this is still what he planned to tell her—but for 'C.'"

Seward was ice.

"May I suppose that you have 'C,' too, Mr. Moon?"

"Yes, Mr. Seward, you may. It is not in itself, however, of a documentary nature. Can any of you truly grasp the blackmail of revenge? The higher animals—I refer to ourselves, to human beings—have used it in varying forms throughout the ages. Any long-drawn-out torture covers the idea: the effects whipped up by the Spanish Inquisition, by our earlier Redskins, by our more current gangsters, in other words by Man. Withholding a glass of water just beyond reach of a victim parched and dying from thirst is perhaps the simplest of the effects I mean. Well, that confession was Myron Jettwick's glass of water, with Mrs. Jettwick and Bruce being the parched victims, of course."

"It was to be ours," Mrs. Jettwick said, "only after he had died?"

"Oh no. If that had been his plan he would have been alive today. There was still his soul, you see."

"No, Mr. Moon, I do not see."

"I'm sure that you will. You, Mrs. Jettwick, and your son were only part of his sins. I speak naturally of those he committed against you. If he had white-washed his soul simply through a confession of those, it would still be black. He had other offenses that required confession, too."

I damned the heat which was making my head dizzy and tried to reduce Moon's chatter to an even simpler form than his ABCs. Okay. Heel Jettwick wanted to torture his ex-wife and nephew right up to within the last few moments of his death, or maybe hours or maybe days. Then, to save his soul, he'd release his confession and exonerate them, after having had the pleasure of watching them stew. He would also release a confession as to his other sins, and so ride up to heaven in a clean white sheet. So he thought.

"Consider," Moon was saying, although how he could keep on talking in that torrid air was more than I could understand, "the number of people who were partially familiar with Myron Jettwick's intentions to purge his soul. All of you who were invited on the cruise knew it. His doctor, his lawyer, his minister, his secretary knew it. And the former wife of Senator Blackman knew it. In fact, you, Mrs. Smith, and your husband were, I believe, the only two people who didn't know it. And now, Mrs. Schuyler, shall we discuss real estate?"

Mrs. Schuyler looked, if I may say so, as dead as mutton, and I've always heard that that's as dead as anything can look. She stayed in the ring, however, even though her voice and her actions did seem under the influence of some remote control.

"Isn't it," she said, "a trifle hot? Why don't you discuss it, Mr. Moon, if it appeals to you as a topic?"

I knew that Moon considered most real-estate operators on a par one shade this side of horse thieves, and prepared for the worst, but he stayed nice, very impartial, very academic and very, very nice.

"Real estate can be fairly dirty at times, and in the Staten Island plan it was rather much so. I refer, Mrs. Schuyler, to the one in which you and Myron Jettwick were mutually interested and in which you had sunk the largest part of your fortune."

Moon's glance gathered the rest of us into this confidential exposé on the doings of big business.

"It wasn't just a question of buying up some lots and developing them with houses and then selling them at a profit. It involved great tracts of land bordering the secret route of a proposed trunk highway which would terminate at a vehicular tube linking Staten Island with Manhattan."

"Fantastic!" said Miss Jettwick. "Although when you think of the Golden Gate Bridge—"

"So would the Hudson tubes have sounded fantastic, Miss Jettwick, not so many years ago, or the Empire State Building or the brevity of Hughes' flight around the world. It was a real-estate promoter's dream: a beautiful suburb brought within swift distance of Manhattan's teeming downtown business section, with an almost unlimited fortune in the pockets of the promoters who brought it to pass. A dream so big that even Myron Jettwick was unable to tackle it alone and had to enlist Mrs. Schuyler to help him. Shall I take up some of the unpleasanter essentials to such a scheme, Mrs. Schuyler?"

"If you wish," Mrs. Schuyler said tightly.

"Shall we touch on the bribery of politicians and of men in high office whose advance knowledge of that secret route was of required value, a bribery that you and Myron Jettwick had already gone in for to the extent of a good large sum? On the fact that all of that bribery was to be brought out, too, by Mr. Jettwick in this purging of his soul?"

"All right," Mrs. Schuyler screamed, "I stole that box. I threw it in the river."

She started to tremble. I started to tremble. The table started to tremble, while a crackling hiss like wind was in the air, but the heat-baked palm fronds did not stir. Moon was white.

"Earthquake," he said.

TWENTY-THREE

THE MAN BEHIND THE DOOR

The light temblor was not repeated. A hush gripped the island and the sea, gripped every living thing, and the sun lost its orange look and deadened to the color of a dark ripe plum. I had a mad mental picture of young Kenny Mattson almost falling to pieces from sheer joy.

Warrenby Dorset was the lad who took command. He knew these little tropical upsets if ever a man did. He pushed his chair back and stood up in the unnatural haze that hovered over the patio floor. We must go at once to the yacht, he said, in a voice that screeched like a foghorn through the incredible stillness of the sky and earth. We must put out to sea and do what we could to outrun the storm, a feat which he thought possible if we were to cast off within the hour.

He was himself prepared to stay, and the black people would stay, too, but he refused, he said, to be responsible for the safety of the rest of us, as our sure salvation lay upon the water.

His loud voice and the sheer melodrama of his statements gave me the first and welcome chill of the day. In regard to the body of McRoss, he said, Moon and Seward could do what they liked. He could either leave it in the house, where the authorities were supposed to examine it before it was moved, or some arrangements could be made to care for it aboard the yacht.

If the center of the disturbance passed over the house, there would be no house left to shelter it. He and the black boys would secure themselves in a small cellar that was prepared for just such an emergency, and would salvage whatever they could of value after the fury of the storm had been spent.

There was suddenly no more day.

A rain that was, but believe me, torrential poured down out of the blackened sky as the advance lash of the storm broke on Tortuagas. Nobody remembers much of what happened during the next hour. The male drowned rats got the female drowned rats on board *Trade Wind*, and then brought down McRoss's body wrapped in the bed sheets. We even hauled luggage, groping blindly through the solid whip of rain, stumbling, sweating, and cursing a path through the obstacles of the storm. We were finally lined up in the main saloon with our noses stuck against the portholes, watching a vague blotch on the dock that must have been Dorset, because his voice shouted something unintelligible up to the bridge, and the landing ladder was raised, the lines cast off and *Trade Wind* heeled shudderingly out for the open sea.

There was only one idea in what was left of everybody's head: to get to a cabin and into dry clothes. That wasn't as simple as it sounds, for all of us were doing a Virginia reel at the will of the bounding floor. Pairs were formed on the old-fashioned theory that the gentlemen would assist the ladies down the companionway and deposit them, preferably intact, at their cabin doors on the deck below.

Moon coupled with Miss Jettwick after signaling me to take care of my charge. Seward offered his arm to Mrs. Schuyler, but then thought better about it and took a firm hook around her waist. Bruce did the handsome with his mother and Elizabeth and, I understood later, between them, they managed to get him safely to his door. I must say that Mrs. Smith looked at me suspiciously when I staggered alongside to take her in tow. I refuse to admit that she shied. All she said was:

"On the feet this time, Handsome. On the feet."

So Mrs. Smith and I bounced, curtseyed and rolled our way below as the motion of *Trade Wind* increased. The boat would slant, quartering up a sea, and hang suspended on a crest; then plunge with a groaning crash flat into the trough with a force that would almost break her and Mrs. Smith and myself in two.

The passageway on the cabin deck was pitch-dark which led me to the bright conclusion that the lighting system had fallen before the storm for the count of ten. I counted, by the sense of touch, the cabin doors as we passed them, and my nose told me when we had reached Mrs. Smith's. I opened it and we hurtled inside.

The cabin swam in furniture and murk, but at least there was murk, and the general outlines were plain enough to be identifiable. Mrs. Smith put her lips close to my ear, from where we were sitting on the floor, and said:

"Listen, Prince Charming, I have had a busy day. I am wet, I am cold, I am bruised all over, thanks both to you and this restless ocean. For God's sake go get me a drink, and try to get back here with it without breaking your neck. I need that drink."

I again found myself under way, and finished the course down the passage like a piece of popcorn that has just fluffed white. Moon, as I might have expected, was calm, cool, and perfectly vertical in the midst of our possessions and the general furnishing of the suite. I said, as I shuffled-off-to-Buffalo past him:

"Mrs. Smith wants a drink. I'm going to take some of your Demerara rum."

Of course he couldn't hear me through the shriek of the storm, but he smiled calmly out of the murk and, for some reason or other, gave my exit into the bedroom a round of applause. I got a bottle of rum from his steamer trunk and waved it at him as I flew past on the return trip to Mrs. Smith.

Her cabin seemed lighter when I reached there, even though the seas slashed a solid wall of water across the ports, turning the place into a purple darkness until the sea fell back. She was sitting on the bed, holding herself there by gripping the footrail. She had taken off her wet clothes and was wrapped in a woolen bathrobe, damp at its neck from the water still dripping from her hair, which was far from being arranged off the face. I shouted:

"Here's the rum, Mrs. Smith," and sat down beside her and started to peel the foil cap from the bottle.

Then I took another quick look at her eyes and got that feeling. They were very set and expressionless, and the smile on her lips was very set and expressionless, too. In fact she looked like a stand-in for one of Madam Tussaud's better waxworks. Anybody who's ever had that feeling will know what I mean. The feeling that somebody was around who shouldn't be around. Who shouldn't be around because, by his being so, he was there to do you no good.

Nobody knows what it comes from, I guess, but it starts with a quiet, cold prickle at the base of the neck and then fans down the spine like a needle spray of ice.

"Hustle up with that cork, Mr. Stanley," she shouted good and loud. "Then beat it out of here because I want to dress."

The "Mr. Stanley" confirmed the feeling. Mrs. Smith had called me practically everything under the sun, but never that. She couldn't have flashed a surer danger signal if she'd turned a bright red.

"Don't be impatient, Heartthrob," I shouted back, which was my way of letting her know that I was on, as never, never had I called her anything but Mrs. Smith, and certainly not to her face.

Well, the lead foil was off the bottle by then and it seemed a good plan to take a few minutes and size things up, so I ignored the corkscrew which is always in my pocket on a sterling silver horseshoe dingus engraved: To Bert from the Duchess; she being a good-hearted old waterfront tramp who would drop in at Harrigan's for a beer whenever she had a dime, and would get one on me whenever she didn't and cut up for thousands when she died, including willing me the sterling dingus and her thanks.

"I have," I shouted, "no corkscrew. Am I dumb!"

"Yes," shouted Mrs. Smith. "Go and get one."

"Nonsense," I shouted. "My old bartending days taught me many a trick. Watch this."

She looked at me as if I really were dumb while I pounded the bottle with the heel of my palm to force out the cork and sized things up. Nobody could hide under the bed, unless it was a snake, and Mrs. Smith would have told me so if it had been a snake. Nor was there anything bulky in the cabin that a man could crouch behind, even if it would stay still long enough for him to do so. Which brought my casual eye to the bathroom door. It was ajar about an inch. What was more, that inch stayed put.

Common sense told me that no door was going to act like that, what with everything else doing Big Apples, unless somebody was holding it there steady.

I caught, even in that one casual glance, what looked like the small muzzle of a gun and again common sense told me it was being held on Mrs. Smith and that she was slated to receive lead if she made one false move.

Any more corkscrew gag was out. You couldn't leave her there to get one, because Annie Oakley would certainly have polished her off and then vanished into his usual mist. Even if I had waited for him outside in the passageway my charge would be dead inside, and this time no fooling.

Strategy, Moon insists, is not one of my major points. A lot of the bulldog, he says, yes; loyalty, a pile-driver technique, yes; but strategy, no. That is just nonsense, of course, and he only says it because he wouldn't want me to get a swelled head. The situation certainly called for finesse, and my plan was to slam Mrs. Smith flat on the floor, then charge the bathroom door and shoot it out, while trying to make the first part of the move look as natural as I could. So I shouted at her:

"Look, Honey Bunch, I guess I've lost the answer. Maybe there's a corkscrew in the bathroom."

With which I slammed her flat.

Well, everything would have been in order if Mrs. Smith's reflex actions hadn't made her rip out a good workmanlike curse and grab my ankle as I leaped across her toward the fray. I realized later that the poor woman was simply tired out from too many unexpected contacts with floors and was in no condition to reason things out.

I did do the best I could, by rolling over and reaching for my gun, but a voice from behind me shouted: "No, no, Mr. Stanley! Stand up and raise your hands, please, and put the palms flat against the bulwark." Now possibly in a reasonable sort of storm you could put your palms flat against the bulwark, but right then no matter when you reached for a bulwark it left you, as did anything else.

I tried the next best thing, which was a sort of patty-cake arrangement and, again, not very good for my nose. It satisfied Voice, however, because he staggered closer and ripped the gun from my hip pocket. His frisking me for further weapons had a touch like Gorilla Larsen's at my favorite Turkish bath, the one in Stockholm where they pound you on a marble dais.

"All right, Mr. Stanley. Sit down."

I did this with ease, after turning around and getting a shock that must have lopped years from my life. I'd been talking with the guy only a couple of hours before in his home on Long Island by radio-telephone. That in itself was one reason why I refused to believe it was Wallace Emberry. The other was because his old-school neatness was lost in a soggy pulp of clothing and matted soil and leaves that seemed to cake in a crust all over him. His pan was streaked with dirt, and there was a jungle smell about him instead of the usual scent of lavender.

I had landed alongside of Mrs. Smith when I sat down, and she said, "Sorry, Old-Timer," and I said, "Forget it, Mrs. Smith," so we were back on a normal basis again.

Not that it looked like doing us much good. Emberry was braced against the wall across the cabin from us, and the gun which he held ready to plug us with had a silencer on its end.

You could tell he was thinking how best to lay us out, to plant some doubt as to how it had happened, to repeat, if he had to, the murder-suicide setup he'd used with Mrs. Smith and McRoss, possibly with her being the suicide this time and me the murdered corpse. He sidled around us rapidly and locked the cabin door; then returned and braced himself again against the opposite wall.

Just then the tail of my eye caught the handle of the door he'd just locked turn, stop, then turn quickly three times. There wasn't any follow-up knock so I knew it was Moon. I knew, too, that he'd got the fact that I was in a spot, and would make some play to get me out of it if any man could. I tried to fight for time, in order to give Moon time. There was always the last chance, of course, of slamming Mrs. Smith flat once more and plowing into Emberry with the hope of getting him before his lead would slow me down.

"Listen, Mr. Emberry," I shouted, "let's bargain."

The idea seemed to interest him. At least he listened while I talked. I talked for five minutes, and I swear I don't know how my tongue did it to this day. I promised him a fair trial in the States. I pointed out how clever he himself had been at criminal law.

I argued that with his money he could get the best mouthpiece in the country. It was all a lot of prize Westphalian bologna, but he listened, at least he didn't shoot, and, even if he wasn't paying any attention, my voice did keep his mind from solving the suicide-murder setup too quickly.

The motion of *Trade Wind* was still wild, but you could tell that Captain Plummet was holding her on the best point to keep her from wallowing over in the mountainous seas. My tongue started to dry up, which sunk my hopes down to a new low, even though I should have known that Moon would dope out the one trick that would have worked. Emberry had it set by then—you could tell that from his eyes—and I was just ready to stake everything on a lunge, when Moon persuaded Captain Plummet to shoot the works.

Trade Wind veered sharply and took one broadside sea.

It was a brilliant piece of seamanship, bringing her back, but Plummet did it, and during that sickening moment while she keeled on her side every movable thing aboard her was in the bag.

That included my gun and Emberry's gun and Emberry.

TWENTY-FOUR

AFTER THE STORM

Trade Wind reached Key West by four in the afternoon. We had left the storm area behind, with its path curving out to sea, but four things made it necessary for a layover in port of several days.

McRoss's body had to be turned over to the Florida state authorities and held for an inquest on his death, after which Miss Jettwick wanted it prepared for burial and to be brought with us back home.

Buzzard Emberry also had to be turned over to the authorities, arraigned and put in jail until it was decided which of his three murders he was to be tried for, or all of them, and when and where. You could also add his attempted strangulation of Mrs. Smith and his later intentions to blast both her and me, after which the civil courts could get busy if they wanted to for odds and ends in malpractice, chicanery, and bribery to the right and to the left. He was, in fact, one of the most all-round villains I had ever known, and the smell of lavender has always given me the jumps from then on.

Trade Wind's superstructure had to undergo quite a few vigorous repairs from damage by the storm.

Lastly, all of us on board her had to undergo some similar vigorous repairs, both of a physical and mental nature, which could best be accomplished on the welcome solidity of dry land.

We checked in at an attractive joint on the waterfront, complete with swimming pool, sweet-smelling flowers, all of the fancier palm trees, a good bar, when you got to see it through the blaze of chromium and mirrors, and a worried, nail-biting manager who looked on our party as a godsend and signed us up at twenty-five bucks a day each. We had, of course, the whole place to ourselves.

As the joint was run on the American plan, the first thing we naturally had to do was to have a dinner party, which Miss Jettwick wanted to sling, somewhere else. She wanted, bless her, to take our minds off our recent worries, which seems a mild way of tabbing same. The manager was delighted almost to death, as it not only saved on the meals, but gave the cook a night out, and suggested that we go to Raoul's Garden of Scented Roses where, he said, shrimps were shrimps. I phoned the orders through to Raoul, who was also almost delighted to death, and said we'd meet the first shrimp at eight. Then I submerged in a good cold tub and slept for two hours.

The dinner party turned out fine. The girls had all freshened up into human beings again, and I had collared a valet in time to have a white mess jacket pressed back into shape. Moon simply raised his eyebrows when he saw me and went right on getting into his sober black.

It wasn't a dinner party so much as it was a minor convention, because Miss Jettwick had invited the officers and men of *Trade Wind* to join us, too. We sat at small tables in Raoul's, which was located just outside of town.

Why he called it Garden of Scented Roses I never did find out, as there were no roses, and all the smells were on the tuberose and gardenia order and they certainly smelt.

There were plenty of trimmings such as stars in the clear, dark sky, very good daiquiri cocktails, languorous dusky waitresses rigged out in straw this side of a hula, and a rumba band of Cubans with their usual effect of hot-syrup strings and loose teeth.

Miss Jettwick and District Attorney Seward sat with Moon and me and Moon gave them a brief *précis* of the case while we ate shrimps and shrimps, and the other tables grouped, danced, drank, and had themselves a time.

"That business about the sapucaia nuts," Moon said, landing a pun below the belt, "was the kernel of the case. If you accepted Bruce's innocence, which I did, the picture of the killer required certain characteristics which were a familiarity with *Trade Wind*, a knowledge of Myron Jettwick's intention to confess publicly his sins before he died, and a fair knowledge of medico-legal procedure. I mean by that, Miss Jettwick, a knowledge specifically of post mortems, which Emberry had from his early practice in criminal law."

"But when you considered his present position in the bar association, Mr. Moon, how could you have suspected him?"

"Nowadays? When governors are being impeached? Just consider the men in high positions of trust who have fallen recently and it becomes feasible to suspect anybody."

"Yes, I suppose it is."

"Emberry knew that he had to kill your brother from the moment the holiday cruise was planned and the invitation was sent to Mrs. Jettwick and Bruce to join it. He saw in Bruce a perfect suspect for the crime. He sought some definite evidence which would plant Bruce at the scene of the crime while, presumably, the victim was still alive. Hence that fiendish and too clever business with the sapucaias."

Moon smiled at Seward and said:

"Both of us knew, Mr. Seward, that your main purpose in establishing the fact that no sapucaias could have been stolen from Bruce on the yacht was to force him into a confession should he have been guilty. I'm sure you knew as well as I did that the nuts could have been taken before Bruce came aboard. Both McRoss and Emberry had an opportunity to do so when they went to Mrs. Jettwick's apartment to persuade her to accept the cruise invitation."

"That will clinch premeditation, of course," Seward said.

"Exactly. New Year's Eve offered Emberry a perfect moment for the crime, with the night watchman of the landing stage drunk and the deck watch drunk. One point, I think, might be enlightening to your case. Primarily, Emberry stood on the aft-deck, after telephoning Bruce, to observe Bruce's reactions through the open porthole. He was detained there, however, after Bruce had gone, by some revelers returning to Wharf House. When he looked again into the bedroom he saw Mrs. Schuyler standing there with the black steel box in her hands."

"How had she located it?"

"During a brief conference with Jettwick before dinner. The box, then, was on a table in the living room, but she had noticed through the open bedroom door that the books on botany were not on the shelf and realized that the space offered a good hiding place for the box."

"Was she dressed for the street then?"

"Yes. Her intention was to take the box ashore and leave it at her house. Finding Jettwick dead naturally shocked her terribly. She took the box into her cabin, feeling faint from shock. She knew that she would shortly be unconscious and didn't dare risk being found with the box in her possession. She managed to throw it into the river through a porthole before she fainted. She remained in this coma until the sailor's shout brought her to, which was why her hat was still on when she first opened her cabin door. She was still confused, and had forgotten the hat and her costume until she saw Mrs. Jettwick looking at her speculatively."

"Emberry saw her get rid of the box?"

"Of course, hence the dragging expedition in the rowboat after it."

"Can we prove he himself was in the rowboat?"

"Yes. Mr. Stanley gave me a very detailed account of that operation. He said that one of the men had removed his mittens in order to draw a gun. This man had also fended the rowboat away from *Trade Wind*'s side with his bare hand. I was certain he had left both fingerprints and palm marks on the yacht's paint. One of Jimmy Singer's men dusted with powdered graphite and then photographed them the following day. They were Emberry's. I'll turn them over to you when we get to New York, Mr. Seward."

You could detect a faintly acid touch in Seward's "Thank you very much."

Moon told Miss Jettwick of our method of having retrieved the box.

"Mr. Seward," he said to her, "was also informed of this by me immediately after the murder of Jeffry Smith. I told him of certain papers I had removed from the box before having it thrown back into the river. They included Jettwick's confessions for his numerous sins. They opened up the field of suspects disturbingly. They gave Emberry a motive for the crime in that they exposed his part in planning the *Leviathan* thefts, in engineering the divorce, and also showed his hand in the general list of bribery and corruption of officials throughout the later years of Jettwick's operations in big real estate. They gave Mrs. Schuyler a motive on similar lines; specifically, of course, the Staten Island project. They gave several powers in the city and state administrations motives, too. This last angle also gave me a lever with which to bargain with Mr. Seward."

Seward's face remained politely interested but perfectly blank.

"The case became too diffuse. I thought it best to smoke Emberry out into the open. I hoped that the ten-thousand-dollar reward would start things going. It was a tempting bait for Emberry's accomplice in the rowboat expedition to turn state's evidence. It was a tempting bait for anybody familiar with Emberry's criminal side or his unethical side. As, for instance, Jeffry Smith had been familiar with it."

"Who was his rowboat accomplice?"

"His servant Plymouth, Miss Jettwick. Plymouth also was to cover Emberry's alibi for the murder of McRoss and the attempted murder of Mrs. Smith by taking phone calls at the estate on Long Island as Emberry, while Emberry was flying down to Tortuagas and back."

"Emberry had some hold on him?"

"Yes. Jimmy Singer 'borrowed' a silver tea service which Plymouth had polished and got his fingerprints from that. His record showed that he was wanted on a ten-year-old murder charge in Buffalo. He had been immune from suspicion, of course, while in Emberry's service, due to Emberry's standing and position."

"How did Mr. Emberry know that Jeffry Smith was about to give you information concerning the divorce?"

"He had kept in general touch with Smith's movements, as he had with those of Mrs. Jettwick and Bruce. He knew as soon as the ten-thousand-dollar reward appeared that Smith might possibly jump for it.

He put Plymouth on Smith's tail. Plymouth overheard from an adjoining booth Smith's phone call to me and drove Emberry to the bar on Fifty-fourth Street. The getaway was most simple, because of the blizzard and the general lack of pedestrians on the street."

"He was then afraid that Mrs. Smith would talk, too?"

"Very much so, which is why Singer had her change her hotel."

"Why didn't you have Mr. Emberry arrested at once. Mr. Moon?"

"There was no definite evidence against him but his fingerprints on the side of the yacht. They proved nothing beyond his presence there and a minor assault on Mr. Stanley's head."

"But the evidence in the box?"

"That proved unethical legal conduct alone, not murder, and would only have resulted in his being disbarred. It also, as I've said, pointed the way to Mrs. Schuyler, in a general fashion to McRoss as a confidential associate in his capacity as secretary and to the men in administration who had been bribed."

"Is that why you arranged the cruise?"

"Yes, with Mrs. Smith frankly being bait. Emberry would feel, as he did feel, that he had to stop her before she talked, and after the yacht docked at Tortuagas was his first chance."

"Why did Mr. McRoss come with him?"

"McRoss knew too much, to a point where Emberry felt the time would come when McRoss would know all. I think that McRoss's death was sealed at the moment when the box was opened before us in the dining saloon, after Commissioner McGilvray had had it brought up. Perhaps you remember McRoss stating that there should be a paper or an agreement concerning the Staten Island project, giving us the impression that he missed other important papers, too?"

"Yes, I do remember that."

"Any reasonable excuse would have served to make McRoss accompany him on the flight down to Key West to join the yacht at Tortuagas. The one Emberry did use was that the missing papers might be found in the house on the island. The murder-suicide setup of McRoss and Mrs. Smith was his plan. Emberry himself, when they landed at Key West, made arrangements for hiring the launch to go over to Tortuagas. He hired it under the name of Jesse Walker, representing himself and McRoss as wealthy sportsmen who had flown down for several days' fishing among the keys. All Southerners think all Northerners are crazy and millionaires and never question their whims or antics."

"How did he persuade Mr. McRoss not to join us immediately when they reached the island?"

"He killed McRoss as soon as they reached the island. There is evidence that he stunned McRoss before he cut his throat. Mr. Seward and I both recognized the fact that McRoss had not been murdered on Mrs. Smith's bed, nor that he could have committed suicide there. His jugular vein had been cut. That causes an almost unbelievable spurting of blood, and there was little, if any, blood on the bed sheets or about the room. On the other hand, when Mr. Stanley captured him in Mrs. Smith's cabin, Emberry's clothes were saturated with blood, wetly so, from it having become loosened by the rain."

"I know he was familiar with the house on Tortuagas. He had been there several times with Myron. But even so, to carry Mr. McRoss's body into Mrs. Smith's room, to strangle her and place the body on the bed—"

"Surely there must have been noise?"

"Not much, Miss Jettwick. Just enough, fortunately, to awaken Mr. Stanley."

I experienced at that point a good hot flush.

"I can see," Miss Jettwick said, "why he felt compelled to follow Mrs. Smith aboard the yacht. He had seen her, of course?"

"Yes. He had watched the whole boarding business from the thick growth along the pathway. It was simple for him to come aboard unnoticed in the blinding rain, the darkness and the complete confusion of the moment. He waited in an empty cabin, the one just across the passage from Mrs. Smith's. He saw her and Mr. Stanley go into her cabin. He saw Mr. Stanley leave it. He did not expect Mr. Stanley to return, although he waited for a moment to see. Then he entered Mrs. Smith's cabin."

"Why wouldn't he have shot her immediately?"

"He had to find out whether she had talked and, if so, to whom. She told him that Mr. Stanley had gone for a drink and would return. He forced her to keep still during Mr. Stanley's return under threat of shooting both of them instantly if she made any overt move. He felt certain that the yacht would put in at Key West, both to turn McRoss's body over to the state authorities and also for repairs she would be sure to need after the storm. He expected no difficulty in stowing himself away for that short run, and especially under hurricane conditions. Once in Key West he would again become Jesse Walker, take a plane back to New York and be Emberry again. An Emberry who had never left his estate on Long Island."

The shrimps, need I say, were pretty nearly all gone.

"What is more," Moon added, "he would have been secure in his position and no longer in dread of exposure, public disgrace and a complete loss of the wealth, the comforts, and the time-honored standing which he had carved for himself from life. And now, Mr. Seward, I believe you flew down to collect these. Our bargain is at an end, all its conditions having been fulfilled."

Moon took the manila envelope from his pocket and gave it to Seward. Moon had picked it up at the Manning, he later condescended to tell me, just before we had sailed. I never did know just which members of the city and state administrations were involved. Which is, for them, just as well, because, even if Moon does exaggerate the point beyond all reason, I do chat.

Little remains to be said.

Warrenby Dorset joined us before we left Key West. His report on the storm effects at the island was terrific. You got the impression of what had once been a lushly treed paradise having been turned into a shaved pancake. All of which had made Dorset and the black boys very doleful indeed because there was nonsense in a job which called for just sitting about on a pancake. Miss Jettwick settled that by giving the black boys a good bonus and by hiring Dorset to manage her holdings out West.

Also, before we left Key West, the complete story had broken in the nation's press and the Violet Vane Cosmetic Hour was almost delirious in its haste to sign Bruce up again, and at four thousand instead of two thousand a week.

It's a pure waste of breath to say that this sat very well with Mother Schuyler. The Staten Island business was all shot and her dough was shot with it, except for the petty twenty percent she still could haul down from her housings up near Columbia University. *Trade Wind*'s run north was, in consequence, a very different affair, so far as she was concerned, than had been the run down. Not only was young Bruce thoroughly white-washed, but gilded as well, and if Mrs. Schuyler ever once formed herself into a threesome during those moonlight nights on deck, I certainly didn't see it.

I must say, however, that she hovered, because she was right on hand to come gliding out from behind the wheelhouse in order to burst into happy tears and bestow her blessings at the break of the clinching clinch.

Yes, love had its way, and Moon had his thirty thousand bucks, and there was I, packing our things again aboard *Coquilla* with nothing more romantic in view than a run to Guiana after Pekea nuts whose destiny in life was to be boiled by Moon in a soup.